pa
THE PIGEON

GAIL SEEKAMP was born in Jersey, an island near France, which was occupied by the Germans during WWII. Originally a journalist, she has also written for children. Her books include the popular *Brainstorm* series and *The Irish Famine*, co-written with Pierce Feiritear. She lives in Dublin with her husband Pierce and daughter, Katie. Family pets include a 16-year-old cat called Slicer and – recently – a visiting wild pigeon with the name Feathers.

SEAN AHERNE is an artist and an internationally published illustrator. He lives in Leicester, England, with his wife Elaine, son Kirk and daughter Scarlett. As well as drawing and painting from an early age, Seán has always kept racing pigeons. Seán now has around fifty pigeons, together with a very ugly dog called Oscar (a pug-Pekinese cross). Oscar sometimes likes chasing the pigeons, with his partner-in-crime, Scarlett.

Dedications

GS: To Katie, Jan and Niall, book-lovers all
SA: To Scarlett

GAIL SEEKAMP

paddy
THE PIGEON

Illustrated by
Seán Aherne

PIXIE BOOKS

First published in 2003 by Pixie Books
72 Cabra Park, Phibsboro, Dublin 7, Ireland.

Text copyright © 2003 Gail Seekamp
Illustrations copyright © 2003 Seán Aherne

ISBN 0-9543544-1-9

All rights reserved. No part of this publication may be reproduced,
stored in a retrieval system, or transmitted, in any form or by any means
without the prior written permission of the publisher, nor be otherwise
circulated in any form of binding or cover other than that in which it is
published and without a similar condition being imposed on the
subsequent publisher.

While the events and some of the characters in this book are based on
historical fact, others are purely fictional.

Editor: Pierce Feiritear
Typesetting: Artwerk Ltd
Cover illustration: Seán Aherne
Map illustration: Conor O'Brien
Cover design: Jason Ellams
Design consultant: Amo Productions
Printed in Ireland by Colour Books

…A ruined farmhouse looms in the mist. Two soldiers crouch on the floor, inside. One takes a steel-grey pigeon from a basket, the other fixes a message to the bird's leg. They move towards the broken window, to release the bird. But, wait…clump, clump, clump go the sound of enemy boots on the road.

Fear gleams in the eye of the bird. The pigeon struggles to break free. They cannot hold it. They cannot hold it! It shoots skyward, twisting and turning. Gunfire explodes…

Andrew Hughes woke with a gasp. He gripped the armrests of his chair, and sat still as a stone for a few lingering seconds. Anxiously, he scanned the darkening room until his grip relaxed. He saw the dogs sprawled by the cooker. Cups gleamed on the table, ready for tea. This was his kitchen, and there were no soldiers here.

It was that awful dream, again. Always those men in the broken-down farmhouse. Hiding, with the pigeon their only hope… The man shook his head, and rose stiffly from the armchair. Lifting the curtain, he peered into the back garden. Rain whipped the trees, and a shed door banged in the wind, once, twice.

"God help anyone at sea this night," he muttered.

Mr. Hughes and his wife Annie lived in a bungalow in Carnlough, a fishing village on the northern shores of Co. Antrim. Their house overlooked the sea, and Mr. Hughes had seen many a storm in his time. Bitter experience told him this was a bad one.

He pulled on his boots. They felt warm and soft from the heat of the Aga cooker. "Are ye coming, Patch?" he called, taking his coat. The two brown pointers slept on but Patch, a brave little terrier, rose and stretched. Man and dog left the cosy kitchen. Heads bent into the rain, they hurried to the feed shed.

Mr. Hughes scooped corn into a bucket while Patch dashed to the corner, barking and sneezing. "*Out. Out!*" the terrier yapped, in a message for any rat who dared show his face on this – or any other – evening. Patch was a small dog, with big notions. The pointers were lazy and spent all day dozing when they were not out hunting with Mr. Hughes. Patch could not relax if he tried.

Mr. Hughes climbed the step-ladder into the pigeon loft, wheezing loudly. Thirty pigeons blinked as he switched on the cobwebbed bulb. The man poured feed into little troughs and fresh water into drinking bowls. Pigeons fluttered down softly, starting to coo-coo and do twirls and dances on the floor.

"Beauty, Beauty," the man called. High in a nest box, a silver pigeon heard the voice, but stayed on her eggs. Darkness closed in again, as Mr. Hughes wheezed his way back down the ladder.

"Late, always late," one pigeon grumbled.

"Ah, don't be fussin'," said another.

The other birds just gobbled their food, stabbing the trough with their beaks as if they would never eat again.

Beauty flew down for some corn. Her mate took his turn to mind their two creamy-white eggs in the nest bowl. After a while, she picked up some grains and flew back to feed him.

"Crunchy," he said. Then, a look of alarm crossed his face. He felt a tap, tap from inside the first egg. "Beauty!" he exclaimed.

"Your turn," she said, feeding him more seeds.

"Hmm," he sulked. The wind screamed against the loft roof and the pigeons were glad to be inside.

Back in the kitchen, Annie Hughes bustled about. She brewed up a pot from old tea-leaves, and set out food. Sugar, tea and other food-stuffs were rationed because of the war, but Annie made fine nutty-brown bread and her own blackberry jam. As they finished supper, a series of 'pips' on the radio demanded Mr. Hughes's attention.

"Here is the News – and this is Frederick Allen reading it.

The Germans say they have evacuated Rzhev, their stronghold on the Moscow front for the past sixteen months.

In both Central and Southern Tunisia, Allied Forces are keeping up their pressure on the enemy.

Our home-based bombers attacked targets in Western Germany last night and laid mines in enemy waters. News has come out of Berlin showing how well our airmen did in their raid on Monday night…"

'Huh!' blasted Mr. Hughes. This war was not going half as well as those BBC reports made out. He was an ex-army man, a World War I captain. He knew the score. March 1943, almost four years of war, yet this man Hitler was as strong as ever. He was halfway into Russia, for God's sake. And the Japanese were on his side. Mr. Hughes could not sleep at night thinking about it. All those young men fighting in Europe, thousands of them, some of them his neighbours' sons. It made him angry.

"Houl' yer whisht," he roared at the radio.

"Andrew," his wife said, soothingly. "Don't be upsetting yourself."

"I tell you, Annie. Our boys have their work cut out for them. I know the German soldiers. Didn't I fight them? Didn't I live in their country after the war? This man has them brain-washed. They'll fight to the last."

He took a deep breath, while Annie poured a fresh cup of tea. Patch was at the table now, looking for a crust. He nudged his master's hand with a moist nose.

"I wish I was out there, doing something. I'm just too old now," her husband muttered.

"There's always the pigeons," Annie reminded him.

"That's right. Amn't I a paid-up member of the National Pigeon Service?" he said, his face brightening.

Patch barked.

"Sometimes I think that dog understands every word you say, Andrew," said Annie with a chuckle.

Mr. Hughes slipped Patch some bread. Rising to his feet, he walked up to the photos that lined their kitchen wall: a wedding portrait; Annie with a pet dog; his nephew Tommy in front of the loft, holding up Beauty. Mr. Hughes lingered over his pigeon 'permit' which he had pinned up next to the photos.

DEFENCE REGULATIONS, 1939

REGULATION 9.

Number. **3.2.**

PERMIT TO KEEP RACING OR HOMING PIGEONS

To All whom it may concern.

By Virtue of the Powers vested in me under the provisions of Regulation 9 of the Defence Regulations, 1939, I hereby grant permission to the Person named below to be in possession of Racing or Homing Pigeons, not exceeding

..**40**......in number, to be kept (*in open loft*) at ...**THE** **MoyLEEN** **LofTs**....
....

NAME OF HOLDER

Surname..... **HuGHES**...
Christian names....... **ANDREW**...
Registered Postal Address.."..**MoyLEEN**"......**CARNLOUGH**.......................
.....**Co. ANTRIM,** .....**NorTHERN** **IreLAND**..........

Andrew. Hughes
Signature of Holder

Date.**31./7./40**

"There's great pigeons out in that loft, Annie," he said, sinking back into his chair by the cooker. "Great Putman* pigeons. They'll do their bit."

* A strain of pigeon

2

The next day, Mr. Hughes rose bright and early. He ate a fresh egg for breakfast, with slabs of brown bread. His bad mood had blown away, as quickly as last night's storm, and he could hardly wait to get into the loft to check the nest boxes for new pigeon chicks.

"C'mon will ye, Patch!" he called.

Patch had vanished. Unknown to Mr. Hughes, Patch was on a committee which made sure that every dog, on every farm in Carnlough and nearby Glenarm, had news of the war. Many farmers' sons from this corner of Co. Antrim in Northern Ireland had enlisted in the army and merchant navy, but not every home had a radio. At this very moment, as Mr. Hughes was struggling into his cold wellingtons, Patch was at McMullan's farm with the latest news.

Mr. Hughes was not worried about Patch. Up in the loft, he found one fine chick in Beauty's nest bowl. The second egg would probably hatch tomorrow. Beauty was his favourite hen pigeon, with her twinkling eye and sure, strong wings. Her first chick was a big, baldy-looking thing, but Mr. Hughes had high hopes for it.

Back in the kitchen, he gave Annie a full report.

"Paddy. That's what I'll call him. His mother, Beauty, now she's a true Putman. The father's a good middle-distance bird, too, mind. He was third in that race from Wales before the war. Do you not remember?"

"Aye, Andrew. I do," she answered, her mind else-where.

Mr. Hughes did the books for local businesses, but pigeons were his passion. People from across the world bought birds from him at the Moyleen Lofts, Carnlough. His Putman pigeons were originally from a loft in Belgium that he had visited after World War 1. When Hitler unleashed another European war in 1939, Mr. Hughes had signed up for the National Pigeon Service (NPS) immediately. Like thousands of other pigeon fanciers, he felt a patriotic duty to breed and train young birds for the war effort. In return, he got 2 ounces of corn per day for every pigeon in his loft. He was also given a handsome blue-and-gold NPS pin and badge, which he wore on his jacket.

"Andrew," Annie cut in, before he could get too fixed on his pigeon-talk. "Can we take a spin into Carnlough for some groceries? Mrs. Stevens said there might be some oranges in."

"Oranges, is that right Annie?" he said, slipping off his boots again. "It's a while since we had them. We'll head in, so."

Back in the loft, Beauty fussed over her new chick. He had no feathers, but was covered in fine yellow hairs, called down. She nuzzled him with her beak, and fed him a thick yogurt-like food from her crop, or throat. This 'pigeon milk' was very good for wee chicks. Paddy was half-asleep, nodding like an ancient tortoise.

"You're a fine young squeaker,*" Beauty said.

Paddy gobbled more pigeon milk, and shivered. He was quite warm with his downy fur, but wanted to tuck in tight to his mother. The other bird – his dad – was fluffing up straw in the nest bowl to keep the place snug.

* A baby pigeon

A while later, he was woken again by a loud cooing just above him.

"What a lovely wee fella!" a pigeon remarked.

"Paddy's his name," his mother replied proudly.

"He'll have a brother or sister real soon now," added a third throaty voice.

As the first-born 'squeaker' Paddy might be stronger than his new brother or sister, but each bird would have to fight its own corner. Around the loft, more hen pigeons were feeding their new-born chicks. Other birds flew quietly to the loft floor, for a drink and a stretch.

SQUAW-W-W-K…C-C-C-RASH!

The calm loft was suddenly disturbed by violent sounds, rising from the hen-house below. There were more squawks, shrieks, then scuffling and soft thuds as hens tried to escape some horrible enemy. Pigeons rose from their perches in waves of panic. "What's up? What's up?" they called. The pointers burst into angry barks from a locked shed nearby, adding to the fright. Paddy felt faint with shock. The air seemed full of hysterical pigeons.

Patch was trotting down the track from McMullan's farm when he heard the racket. He burst into a gallop. "Must be a rat, must be a rat," he barked. After the committee work, Patch took his rat control job very seriously. He squeezed under the fence at the top of the garden, his eyes flashing. Racing to the hen-house, he scrabbled at the wire. Patch knew a rat had broken in. Where was it now? The dog skidded into the feed shed, sniffing the ground as he went.

"What's the fuss?" shouted Mr. Hughes, appearing with Annie close behind. She looked a bit annoyed, as she wanted to get to the shops.

"Rat, rat," the dog barked. Mr. Hughes knew exactly what he meant.

"Aye, is it a rat, Patch?"

The dog gave a disgusted sneeze. Mr. Hughes came into the feed house, and kicked the two tall drums that he used for pigeon corn. Silence. Nothing scrambled out. From the wild clucking next door, he knew a rat had got into the hen-house. Where was it now?

A rat was well able to climb straight up a stone wall – could it be in the loft? Mr. Hughes shot up the ladder, forgetting his sixty-two years. His arrival triggered another shock wave of pigeons into the air. Recognising their trainer, the birds whirred briefly and landed again. The man moved slowly, not wishing to frighten them. He looked in the nesting boxes, checking Paddy and the second egg. All was well.

Satisfied, he sat on a stool and talked softly to his pigeons. Only when they had almost dozed off did he climb back down the ladder for the trip to the village.

3

Paddy was now a month old, and a different bird. In his first week, he had almost trebled in size and Mr. Hughes had slipped a metal ring onto his leg. The ring felt strange, but his dad said all serious pigeons needed one. It was stamped with his National Pigeon Service number: NPS-43-9451.

He had sprouted white feathers all over his body, with patches of black and charcoal grey. Paddy also slept a lot less. He and his brother, Bouncer, liked hopping around the tiny nest box when their parents were not feeding them corn. Bouncer lived up to his name, being stronger and livelier than Paddy.

"Time to wean you, my lads," said Mr. Hughes one day. The man peered at them, his spectacles perched on the end of his nose. "You look tired, Beauty," he said sympathetically. Beauty had two new eggs. In ten days' time, she would have more squeakers to feed.

"He's got a large beak," said Paddy, staring at the man's nose.

"And look at the shiny things on the end of it!" Bouncer joked.

The brothers had much to learn, starting with this 'weaning' business. Mr. Hughes looked busy. He found a yard brush, and swept out a second loft right beside them. The youngsters gawked as he scrubbed the walls and laid fresh straw on the ground. He disappeared down the ladder and returned with a basket. Rectangular in shape, it was made of thin branches and had small holes cut into one side. He fixed two long dishes under the holes on the outside of the basket.

"What's he doin', Ma?" Bouncer asked.

Beauty preened her feathers, and said nothing.

Bouncer nudged Paddy. Mr. Hughes had finished with the basket. Now, he was looming in front of their nest box. Opening the door, he put a huge hand inside and cupped it around Paddy's body. Skilfully, he slipped Paddy into the basket then returned for Bouncer. He was taking them from their parents!

Soon he had ten youngsters in the basket. Mr. Hughes brought it into the second loft, laying it down as carefully as if it were Annie's finest bone china. He tinkled some grains into one dish and splashed water into the other. Then he left the room, pulling the door shut.

Stunned, the young pigeons crouched still and quiet. Then one voice piped up, "*Squeak. Squeak-k-k!*" After a wee while they were bantering and jostling like the best of friends.

"Look, Bouncer," said Paddy. Poking his head through the hole in the basket wall, he spotted some pale-coloured seeds. He pecked hungrily until Bouncer nudged him aside. Before long, all the pigeons had taken their fill. There was little left to do but relax, so they huddled together sleepily.

When night was falling, Mr. Hughes came back. At the rattle of the seed can, the youngsters woke.

"Here, lads and lassies," the man called, kneeling by the basket with a heavy grunt. A few more seeds spilled into the tray. When the youngsters had pounced on every last scrap, Mr. Hughes opened a side flap on the basket to release them. Rattling the can, he poured a final ration of corn into big dishes on the floor. All the while he spoke softly, admiring each pigeon in turn and stroking its silky back.

Hot-tempered Mr. Hughes was never cross with his pigeons. "The secret with young birds is to feed them well, and be their friend," he used to tell his young nephew, Tommy. "Pigeons who trust their trainer will fly their hearts out to return home."

Morning and night, he repeated the routine. He rattled the feed can to announce his arrival, filled the dishes and handled each pigeon in turn.

One fine evening though, he did something unusual. After coaxing the youngsters back into the basket, he shut it tightly. Heaving it off the ground, he walked back into the big pigeons' loft and re-opened the side flap.

Sun streamed into the loft from a cage-like frame at the entrance that overlooked the garden. Paddy had not noticed it until now. Warm air gushed through the wicker walls of the basket. This was exciting, but the youngsters felt rooted to the spot.

"Time for a walk and a bath," Mr. Hughes announced.

He poured corn into a nearby bowl and whistled quietly. Paddy shot his head out of the basket, jerking his gaze this way and that. Inside, the others shivered.

"Where are we? What's going on?" they cried. "What's that light?"

Snow-Girl, a pure white pigeon, joined Paddy at the open side flap. They both blinked, then dashed over to attack the corn. Eight other small heads poked out of the basket. These pigeons also raced for the bowl.

The young birds were hot and thirsty. A flat tray of water sparkled near the sunlit cage at the front of the loft. One by one, the pigeons approached and splashed in the shallow water, shaking their short wings, showering drops everywhere.

Afterwards, they sat drying in the sun and peered at the world outside. Grown-up pigeons were swooping over Mr. Hughes's garden. They moved in a tight little flock, looping in ever-changing circles, soaring over the sheds and the roof of the house, then darting out of view behind the trees, in no hurry to return. Tiny flies danced in the golden light, twinkling like jewels. It was a perfect Spring evening.

Paddy spotted Mr. Hughes leaving his kitchen. A brown-and-white terrier scurried at his feet. Paddy heard the usual banging and barking from the feed shed as Mr. Hughes collected seed and water and Patch sorted out the rats. The man climbed the ladder, rattling the feed can.

As if by magic, the big pigeons began circling in front of the loft and dropping through the thick bars at the entrance. The rattling of the can was a signal, the young pigeons realised. Time for supper and a cool drink! Paddy and Bouncer gasped as these huge pigeons landed on the boards beside them. They had darting eyes, enormous necks and shoulders. Their feathers had a smooth, shining glow of total fitness. Next to these athletes, the youngsters felt ridiculous with their small bodies and rough, damp feathers. As one giant bird stepped in, Mr. Hughes called:

"Joe-Boy. Here, Joe-Boy."

Paddy glanced at Bouncer. This was the champion racer their mother, Beauty, had spoken of. At that moment, each youngster vowed to be as mighty a pigeon as Joe-Boy. For they were racing pigeons, and this was in their blood.

4

Learning to fly in the small loft was not easy. To make matters worse, Mr. Hughes had brought another dozen birds into this 'junior' section. But it was the only place to practise. Eager youngsters would rise into the air, wings madly flapping, and miss the other pigeons by a feather's breadth.

"Watch out!" they snapped at each other.

Paddy found that springing from his perch was perfect for short flights. His gang was still sleeping in the basket but they roamed the loft by day. Bouncer had been the first to spot the perches that lined the walls. The young pigeons squabbled over who got the highest perch. Usually it was Paddy, but sometimes Snow-Girl got there first.

Mr. Hughes was pleased with their progress. One day, he gave the youngsters a small breakfast and locked them in the basket all day. That evening, he carried them down the ladder and out through the feed shed. The pigeons were starving by now, and scared too.

Mr. Hughes walked into his back garden and put the basket on the ground close to the loft. Then he turned to his helper, a freckle-faced boy who wore a brown cloth cap. "Now, Tommy," he said. "I want these youngsters to fly up to the loft entrance. It's their first time. I'm going back into the big loft. You know what to do. When I give you the signal, let them go."

The boy nodded. Mr. Hughes disappeared into the feed shed. Moments later, he was up in the loft sprinkling corn onto some metal dishes, just behind the entrance. The grains made a hard ringing sound, so loud that the youngsters heard it down in the garden. They scrabbled hungrily inside the basket. Mr. Hughes signalled to Tommy, who started tugging the straps free. The boy opened the side flap, flooding the pigeons with fresh air and light.

They did not hesitate. Tumbling out, the birds rose raggedly into the air as if a dozen cats were chasing them. They crashed into one another, veering to the left and right. Pumping the air with their wings was easy enough, but flying in the right direction was hard. One young bird hit a bush with a loud *crack*; another flew into the feed house. Paddy kept his eyes on the loft opening, landing first. With almighty flaps, each youngster finally reached the loft. Bouncer perched obstinately on the roof for a few minutes, but was tempted in by a rattle of the seed can. They strutted through the bars, ready for their corn suppers and a drink of water.

"Good work," said Mr. Hughes, when all the pigeons were safely locked up. "Time for our supper, Tommy."

As they ate, the boy chatted non-stop, determined to ask his uncle every new pigeon question he could think of. He loved escaping from his tiresome baby sisters to help his uncle train the pigeons. Mr. Hughes obliged, but his concentration seemed to fade after a while.

"Shussh!" his uncle finally snapped, as the radio pips announced the Six O'Clock News.

"Here is the News – and this is Frank Phillips reading it.

In Tunisia, the Allies' steady progress continues. The enemy has been counter-attacking near Medjez El Bab. In the Pont du Fahs area, French forces have

*now completed a fifteen-mile advance. The weather
has interfered with our air offensive but the Italian
base at Bari has been bombed again.*

Our Malta fighters…"

Tommy drank in each sentence, imagining these mysterious places full of battle-hardened soldiers, all trying to kill each other. Medjez El Bab, Pont du Fahs, Bari. It was mind-boggling.

When the News was over, his uncle relaxed again, listening with Aunt Annie to some funny tunes on the 'Orchestra Show'. Tommy got bored, and could not resist another question.

"Uncle," he burst out. "What's the bravest thing a pigeon has ever done in the National Pigeon Service?"

Mr. Hughes smiled patiently. "Well, I knew several pigeons that were dropped into France in the Great War," he replied. "These pigeons were tossed out of planes inside baskets, each attached to a little parachute. The basket also contained food and instructions. Sometimes, French people would find them, and bring them home. If the people had a secret message to send – about the enemy – they'd release the bird."

"And did the pigeons get back to England, Uncle?"

"Yes, often they did, lad."

"Did they save people? In the war, I mean?"

"Pigeons saved hundreds of lives! There was one mealy* hen called Jane. She was on board a sea plane in the Great War of 1914-1918. The plane crashed into the sea, over fifty miles from land, with four crew."

* A mix of brown and white

"And what happened?" quizzed Tommy, his eyes as wide as saucers.

"The crew released Jane with a message on her leg that gave their position in the sea. It said something like: 'Down. All crew OK. Please send help,'" Mr. Hughes said, confidently. "Those messages were top secret, you know. Only the RAF boys got to see them…Anyway, she was home in 53 minutes – after flying almost mile a minute. The crew were all rescued, thanks to brave Jane. And she," he added with a twinkle in his eye, "was Joe-Boy's great-great-great-great grandmother. Or something like that. Another time-"

"Time we got you back to your house, and your homework young lad," Annie cut in, turning to Tommy.

"Aye. That's right, or you'll be no use to me for pigeon-work," joked Mr. Hughes as he rose to look for his coat.

5

Helped by Tommy, Mr. Hughes repeated the garden 'drop' two days later. Soon the youngsters were flying straight from the basket to the loft. They started exercising outside, like the adult birds, but Mr. Hughes always released them just before supper when their hunger was sharpest. Within a fortnight, he had stretched the drop distance to a mile, along the coast.

One evening in May, Mr. Hughes suggested a picnic. "It's going to be a fine day on Sunday, Annie. Do you fancy a visit to Slemish Hill?"

"Why not?" she said. "I wouldn't suppose you'd be bringing a few pigeons along for company, would you?"

"Aye," he admitted. "I thought of bringing young Tommy, his mother and her wee lassies. Perhaps a few pigeons, too."

Sunday was hazy and dry, as the weather-man had promised. Tommy, excited, woke at 7 o'clock and galloped down for breakfast.

"Ma," he said, between mouthfuls. "What's the plan for today?"

"We'll go in two cars to Slemish for our picnic," his mother Angela replied, as she wiped porridge from baby Katie's face. "Your uncle will go back to the loft, in his car. He'll be there, waiting for the pigeons when we let them go."

"And the pigeons, Ma," blurted Tommy. "Don't I get to release the pigeons after Uncle Andrew goes?"

"Your uncle is the person to ask about that, Tommy," she replied.

"Only I can do it, Ma. Haven't I trained them all along? It has to be me!"

Just before noon, they drove to Uncle Andrew's bungalow. It took an age for the grown-ups to finish all their chat and pack the picnic into the cars. They had a feast prepared: home-cured ham, brown bread spread with salty farm butter, crisp Cox's apples and a jar of local honey. There were even two fresh oranges – a rare treat – with a sharp knife to quarter them. The adults had a paraffin stove, too, for making their tea.

Tommy helped lift the pigeon basket onto the back of his uncle's sky-blue Rover. Mr. Hughes looked very smart, with his plus-fours and red leather boots. "Sit in there, Tommy," he said. "Just a light breeze, and no risk of rain, mist or fog. Perfect weather for their first serious flight."

The cars ground out of the driveway and turned right on the coast road to Glenarm village. Craggy cliffs rose from the road, over-looking a sparkling sea. At Glenarm, just by the church, the road swept up the valley towards Slemish Hill. It was under ten miles to Slemish from Carnlough by car, but barely five miles as the crow – or pigeon – flew. At last the cars pulled off the road below Slemish Hill. Tommy had a big smile on his face; he had struck a deal with his uncle.

The adults and children unloaded the picnic baskets, and hiked up the hill to a sheltered spot that overlooked the valley below.

"Look, there's the sea," yelped Tommy.

"Can you see Scotland, Angela?" Annie asked.

"I'm not sure," she replied.

"Forget Scotland," roared Mr. Hughes. "All the pigeons want to see is their loft!"

Laughing, they spread out blankets for the picnic. When

everybody had eaten their fill, the adults debated where St. Patrick might have lived on Slemish, and whether he used to keep pigeons all those centuries ago. "Aye. He might have sent one home to Wales with a message!" Mr. Hughes quipped.

Meanwhile, Patch chased rabbits and the children chased Patch. After much tearing round in circles, the children and the dog rejoined the grown-ups, all hot and tired. Tommy flopped onto his back, and squinted at the sun for a few seconds.

"Uncle," he said, suddenly. "How do they do it?"

"Do what, Tommy?"

"Pigeons. How do they find their way back to the loft? You know, the ones they let go hundreds of miles from their home. Even in strange countries?"

"That's a very good question, Tommy. Even the scientists aren't sure they have the answer."

"What do *you* think, Andrew?" Annie asked.

"Well, it's hardly just the sun, because pigeons can fly at night, and in fog or snow," her husband replied slowly. "Some people say pigeons see magnetic rays that we don't. They certainly have sharp eyes, make no mistake. And a pigeon may be small, but he's got a mind of his own. I remember one pigeon I entered in a club race from Wales. Didn't see him for three weeks, never showed up. One day, he flies home, fresh as a daisy. What had he been up to? Don't ask me. They're mysterious creatures, pigeons.

"Enough of this chat," he said, suddenly remembering the job they had to do. "Time for me to get back to the loft, and get it ready. It's 2.20 p.m. now. Give me thirty minutes' head start, then release the pigeons. You know the drill, Tommy."

His nephew grinned from ear to ear.

Followed by Patch, Mr. Hughes got into his car. Snapping on the engine, he waved and was off. As he drove home, the man worried about his young birds, as he always did. Today would be a real test for Paddy and the others. 'I hope the falcons aren't out,' Mr. Hughes thought, as he swung into his driveway. 'What would I say to Tommy?'

Back on Slemish Hill, Tommy counted the seconds, as if they were hours. His mother checked her watch, but still they waited. Finally, she nodded at Annie.

"It's almost ten to three now, Tommy," Annie said. "Time to let them go."

Together, they heaved the basket onto a long slab of granite rock. Tommy struggled with the stiff leather straps, and then the pigeons were free. With a great surge, they were off.

6

Up, up they climbed with a furious beating of wings. Tommy, and even the battered old car, soon became specks on the mountain, far below. The boy seemed to be waving his cap, but it was hard to make him out. The brown cliffs of Slemish and its twin peak, Carragin Hill, dropped away steeply as the ten pigeons veered north-east, towards the sea and Carnlough.

Paddy felt the soft, powerful air pummel his wings. It felt magical. Below him, the bare rock gave way to rough grassland and heather. Next came brightly-coloured fields, divided into a patchwork of shapes by fat green lines. Rectangles, ragged squares and scraps of garden, in all shades of green. This valley had been gouged out by a glacier thousands of years ago, long before pigeons or men had lived in these lands. Now houses dotted the hill slopes, and sheep grazed peacefully.

"Wheee-ee-ee!" shouted Paddy. "Wheee-ee-ee," replied his brother. Soon all the pigeons were calling to each other.

Whoosh. Whoosh, went their steady wing-beats. It was not as if one pigeon chose the way home, somehow they all knew. They flew in a tight flock at first, carefully following the road that led seawards. Then the fun started, as the pigeons started to dip and dive without warning.

"ZZZZ," said Bouncer, dropping like a stone. He narrowly missed a few heads. The other birds copied, tumbling like clowns. They discovered that the air had different currents, some warm and some cool. It was easier

to shoot upwards on a draft of warm air, and plunge downwards on a cold one.

The green fields were replaced by more rock and two small hills that were set apart but exactly the same height. The air was colder here, the flying harder. The pigeons cut like a stream of arrows through the narrowing valley, skimming Ticloy Hill to their left. Thick pine trees covered the foot of the hill.

"Let's stop at the trees," shouted Bouncer. "I'm tired."

"No!" cried Paddy, veering towards him. "Home. Mr. Hughes is waiting."

Fearing his brother would land them in trouble, Paddy led the flock with Snow-Girl. She set a cracking pace, with the pigeons racing to keep up with her. Before long, Jane took the lead. Not to be outdone, Bouncer tore past next. He was no longer tired.

Moments later, a sliver of light glinted below, reflecting the sun like a broken mirror. It was the Glencloy River, which flowed towards a ragged coastline. But first came a cluster of houses. They had reached Carnlough.

Flying as one, the pigeons saw the church spire and the painted faces of the village shops. They swooped over McNeill's grocery and the hotel near Carnlough's busy harbour. Their loft was now close. They had been flying for about twelve minutes, but it seemed like seconds. 'I want more,' thought Paddy.

Mr. Hughes was in the loft, waiting for his birds. He fussed over the feeding bowls, checked his watch and went down into the garden. Squinting at the sky, he saw specks appear on the horizon. The tiny shapes grew larger, more distinguishable. Strange. This was a very large flock. And where was Snow-Girl, his white hen?

He grew more and more uneasy. Something was wrong; this was not his flock. It must be another one, perhaps out training. If his youngsters got caught in this group, he would lose them. Mr. Hughes felt his heart sink.

"No! No!" he shouted, waving his arms frantically.

Zipping through the air, Paddy suddenly saw the loft's grey slate roof. A split second later the other flock surged towards them. All in an instant, the two flocks mixed together like a pool of liquid, with Mr. Hughes's birds dragging to the back. The older birds were flying hard and fast, and the tired youngsters could barely keep up. Their loft roof flashed by, as they dipped over the nearby hill towards O'Grady's place. They did not hear Mr. Hughes shouting, nor did they see his arms rotating like windmills. Their hearts beat like train wheels on a track. Familiar landmarks were slipping away. The youngsters had been sucked into this other flock of racing birds, and they could not get free.

Below them, unaware of this drama, was Patch. He was heading for O'Grady's farm to see Captain, the big sheep-dog. As he trotted along the path, Patch growled the latest bit of War News, trying to remember the details.

"Italy. Mussolini's men. Northern France. Bomb attacks on…"

He turned into the yard, but Captain was not at his usual spot by the front door. The back yard was also quiet, except for a few nasty-looking cats and some hens scratching in the dust.

'Hmm,' thought Patch. 'What now?'

Sniffing the air, he spotted a large flock of racing pigeons streaming above the yard. At the back was a small, pure-white bird. "Snow-Girl," he barked once. Then, like a dog who had lost his mind, he barked again and again: "SNOW-GIRL!...SNOW-GIRL!...SNOW-GIRL!"

The shrill yaps rising from the ground could not be ignored. Paddy looked down and saw a small brown-and-white terrier jumping in a frenzy. Patch!

"Snow-Girl, Bouncer, Blue," Paddy called.

At his signal, the young pigeons began to sweep away from the bigger group, the spell now broken. They saw Patch more clearly. In the distance, Paddy spied the roof of their own loft. Home!

Minutes later, the tired youngsters fluttered onto the landing board. Mr. Hughes was waiting inside, topping up the trays with light pigeon seed. "Come, come," he called softly. "You're back. Here's a lovely supper for you."

He sat on the ground and stroked each bird, one by one, calling its name and speaking in a low voice. Then he checked their wings for any injuries, gently stretching out the feathers. "Good boy, good girl," he said.

7

Mr. Hughes was exhausted. When he had finished with the pigeons, he sank in his comfortable armchair by the cooker and into a troubled sleep.

The farmhouse, again. Three soldiers on the ground, or is it two? The Germans are coming back. Time to free the pigeon. But where is it? Not in the basket. Is it outside? No, there's a falcon circling in the air, swooping in menacing circles. Round, and round, and round…

"Cup of tea, Andrew?" Annie said, bursting into his dream. Her kind voice chased it away and brought her husband back to the snug kitchen. Mr. Hughes was glad to be awake. He switched on the radio, and reached for the tea. It was hot, and refreshingly sweet.

"That was a close thing, Annie," he said. "We nearly lost those young pigeons today. They need more training."

"Aye. That'll be no trouble to you," she replied.

"True, but the RAF boys want them soon."

Patch woke, hearing their voices. He thumped his tail on the mat. Time for a well-deserved crust, perhaps with a dollop of jam? But his master ignored him and started shuffling through a jumble of papers on the window-ledge.

"Here, take a look at this, Annie," Mr. Hughes said, handing an open envelope to his wife.

Arranging her glasses on the tip of her nose, she took out the letter and read:

National Pigeon Service

May 10th, 1943

Dear Sir,

Members of the NPS are required to provide pigeons immediately for the War Effort. Young birds are now urgently needed for coastal protection work at three RAF stations in Northern Ireland. Mature birds also gratefully accepted.

Please contact Sergeant Drew (092) 6417 to arrange collection before end May.

Yours truly,

Sergeant S Drew

Head of National Pigeon Service,
Northern Ireland

8

Mr. Hughes was on the phone the very next morning.

"Sergeant Drew," he said. "Andrew Hughes here. Moyleen Lofts, Carnlough."

"Aha, Mr. Hughes," Sergeant Drew replied. He knew the name well.

"I got your letter," Mr. Hughes went on. "I've some fine young pigeons for you."

"Wonderful," the officer shouted. "How many?"

"Ten in this lot, perhaps more later," Mr. Hughes replied, holding the phone away from his ear.

"Are they trained, Sir?" barked the sergeant.

"A bit more to do," Mr. Hughes replied crisply.

They arranged the details. Sergeant Drew said that other members of Mr. Hughes's local pigeon club, the Ballymena & District Homing Society, were also supplying pigeons to the NPS. He asked if these birds could be dropped at Moyleen Lofts, and Mr. Hughes agreed.

So, it was all decided. A truck would collect the pigeons in a week's time. They would travel to a Royal Air Force base, probably RAF Ballykelly at the tip of Northern Ireland. Mr. Hughes would get them back after the war – any that survived, that is.

After the call, Mr. Hughes rang his NPS friends. Next, he got a sheet of paper and a sharp pencil. 'Time to get those youngsters into shape,' he thought.

Patch scrabbled at the door, eager to get to Carnlough to give his latest update. "Away with you," said Mr. Hughes

31

opening the door absent-mindedly, then returning to his list.

TRAINING

May 17th, 1943

Monday:	Check rings, flight feathers. Change feed mix. Exercise.
Tuesday:	Glenarm drop
Wednesday:	Rest, check baskets
Thursday:	Slemish Hill drop
Friday:	Short training, obedience work
Saturday:	Twenty-mile drop
Sunday:	Rest, fly-about. Paper-work.

* * * * * * * *

Monday:	Collection (10.30 a.m.)

Before heading out to the loft, he made one more call. This one was to his sister, Angela.

"Would young Tommy stay here this week?" he asked. "We could send him off to school each morning. He could help with the pigeons in the afternoons."

"Of course, Andrew," she replied, warmly. "He'd be delighted. Tommy lives for those pigeons."

The following day, Tommy arrived with a little travelling case. He had packed his toothbrush, pyjamas and some old clothes for the loft. That morning, he had told *all* his friends in school about his uncle and the pigeons. "He needs me to help him," Tommy had told them proudly. "It's for the war, you know."

After tea and cake, Auntie Annie drove the boy and the pigeons down to Glenarm. Tommy liberated the birds in front of the village church as jackdaws circled overhead. With a noisy clamour of wings the pigeons shot away, with Paddy in the lead.

They repeated the same exercise on Thursday, this time from Slemish. The flock returned in record time, despite a thick mist that hung over the Glens.

Mr. Hughes was well pleased. He did not believe in potions and lotions for pigeons, just good food, firm discipline and a few treats. On Saturday, after their twenty-mile drop, he praised the youngsters and slipped tasty seeds into their feeding bowls. Angela also gave Tommy a little surprise after supper. It was parsnip, mashed up with sugar, a taste of butter and drops of banana essence. She called it 'bananas' and Tommy, who could barely remember what a real banana looked like, was thrilled.

"It tastes gorgeous!" he said.

Sunday came all too quickly. After breakfast, Tommy helped feed the pigeons, a job he normally loved. But now he stared glassily as they scampered on the loft floor. A cheeky dark-grey pigeon (Bouncer) pecked his boot, demanding more corn. 'They'll be gone tomorrow,' Tommy thought. He helped his uncle carry the pigeons owned by the Ballymena pigeon men to an empty shed, ready for the morning. Silently, they stacked the baskets against the wall. It was time for church, followed by one of Aunt Annie's mountainous Sunday lunches.

At 4 o'clock, Tommy's mother drove up to the house and

honked her horn. The boy gave his uncle a hurt look. He felt miserable.

"D' ye' want to say a quick good-bye to Paddy and his friends?" his uncle asked.

The boy nodded, and shot out the door. Minutes later he was back, with a twinkle in his eye and loose pigeon feathers stuffed into his pockets. "Can we start training those other young pigeons soon, uncle?" he asked. With that, he was gone, shouting:

"'Bye Uncle Andrew. 'Bye Aunt Annie!"

The house fell strangely quiet with the boy gone. Before supper Mr. Hughes tramped upstairs to get ready for the loft. Instead of getting his work-clothes, he rooted in a trunk next to the bed. Stiffly, he put on an old jacket made of thick felt-like material, and a pair of green trousers to match. This was his World War One uniform, and it was studded with medals and badges. There was even a battered tin helmet, also green, with dents and scratches.

Followed by Patch, he headed for the loft. The young pigeons gasped as the dark green helmet appeared at their door. Standing straight as a pole, Mr. Hughes bellowed:

"BOUNCER, ANJI, PADDY, SNOW-GIRL, JOE, BLUE, MAJOR, TWINKIE, JANE AND PEARL!"

The pigeons popped up their heads. They swivelled round to face him, with startled looks.

"ATTENTION!!" Mr. Hughes said. At that command, they shuffled over to his feet and stood in a ragged line. The man pulled out his three-legged stool. Sitting down, he spoke again in a quieter voice.

"Lads and lassies, he said. "I've news for you."

"Coo-ee," said one of the pigeons.

"You're off to the war!"

The pigeons blinked.

"You're fit, well-trained. Our boys are fighting the Germans, and you've got to do your bit. You're off tomorrow for the adventure of your lives. Do your job, fly safely and you'll come back home – safely."

He pulled a handful of seed from his pocket. As the pigeons scurried around him, stabbing the seed with their beaks, he stroked their backs with his finger-tips. When the food was gone, he told them stories of pigeons who had flown through gunfire and cruel storms to save men's lives, of pigeons who had been shot and wounded, but still made it home. The birds cocked their heads, and exchanged looks. 'I wonder if they understand?' Mr. Hughes thought.

Early next morning, an RAF truck pulled into the back yard. It was full of eager young pigeons, crammed into wicker baskets in groups of eight to ten. They stretched their necks to stare at this new group.

Mr. Hughes helped to load the baskets. Paddy's last sight of Moyleen Lofts, as the truck pulled away, was of a sad-looking Mr. Hughes, and Patch giving a mad yodelling bark by his master's side. As the truck roared down the coast road on its journey north, the pigeons buzzed with excitement. Good-bye Carnlough!

9

RAF Ballykelly looked forbidding. As the truck pulled into the base through a gate set in a taut wire fence, a cold wind whipped over its deserted runways.

Operational flying had almost ceased at RAF Ballykelly since February 1943, when the Liberator planes of the 120 Squadron had moved to England. Now the base was home to visiting Royal Navy planes, and it provided an Air/Sea Rescue Service. Ballykelly's coastal location was perfect for this job but exposed it to very bad weather. The mud flats of Lough Foyle stretched to the north; in the east rose treacherous Binevenagh Mountain. The pilots called it 'Ben Twitch', and feared for their lives whenever they had to negotiate its craggy slopes in low cloud.

A barrel-chested officer shouted at two soldiers to take the pigeons. Cursing, they grabbed a few baskets and took them to some newly-built wooden lofts.

The pigeons pressed together in fear. They thought of Mr. Hughes and his kind voice. This was so different.

Inside the loft, another man opened the side-flaps on each basket. He gave the pigeons food and water, then switched off the light. Suddenly, he was gone. The pigeons were stunned. No exercise. Instead, this man had locked them up!

The next day was the same, and the one after that. For two whole weeks the pigeons were prisoners. All they could do was eat, sleep, make friends and grumble.

"We're good fliers," Bouncer said one day. "We could be

out saving people's lives and…" He paused, stuck for words. "Doing things."

"Doing what things?" Snow-Girl asked.

"Things. Saving people, like Mr. Hughes said," he replied.

"How?" asked Paddy.

In truth, the pigeons did not know. Nor did they realise that this enforced captivity was called 'resettling' and that it was part of their training. If their loftman released them too soon, they might get lost.

Their new handler was a Sergeant McLean from Scotland. He was gentle and calm with them, like all good loftmen. Neither old nor young, he had peppery hair and a serious manner.

One day, he put the ten Moyleen Loft pigeons into their basket and brought them to a small room. Peeking out through the wicker-work, Paddy saw other men sitting with pigeon baskets in front of them. Some had pencils and notebooks at the ready. The barrel-chested man was at the top of the room, about to speak.

"HURR," came a horrible noise from his throat. "HUURRRGGGHH!"

A snigger broke out.

"QUIET!" roared Sergeant Drew, his voice fully recovered. "We're not running a HOLIDAY CAMP here, nor at any other RAF base," he growled. "These birds are now used to the lofts. It's time to get those wings in the air. FROM TOMORROW!

"I'm glad to see some loftmen with notebooks. I want ALL of you to keep DAILY records of training, flying times, et cetera. Some of these pigeons may be needed by the RAF boys in England. We must know who the fittest, fastest and smartest pigeons are!

"After training, this new batch will start rescue work," Sergeant Drew went on. "In the North Channel, between Northern Ireland and Scotland. They'll go out with supply boats and on RAF special missions. Their job is to RETURN TO BASE, with an SOS message, if a boat or plane gets into trouble. Lives will depend on them."

Paddy and others blinked. His message was loud and clear.

That evening, Sergeant McLean did something new. Before supper, he opened the loft's front hatch for the first time. Anxious at first, the pigeons crouched on the landing board staring at the sky. Not Bouncer. He unfolded his wings, and swept in a wide circle over the loft. Soon they were all twisting and turning through the air like acrobats. Flat grey concrete stretched below. They could not see the scented green fields of the Antrim Glens, nor the white-crested sea of Carnlough, but it was good to fly again.

Sergeant McLean began a training schedule that got tougher by the day. He also flew them at strange times and in all sorts of weather, unlike Mr. Hughes.

Once he released them in bitter rain, about fifty miles from the base. The pigeons 'homed', one by one, utterly exhausted. Only Blue failed to return.

"I'm starving," Paddy said, gobbling seeds as soon as he entered the loft that evening. Around him, other hungry pigeons were taking their fill.

"No sign of Blue," cooed Pearl. She was a quiet pigeon, with a pink and silver sheen on her head and neck. Blue and Pearl were good mates.

"He stopped off for a nap," Bouncer wise-cracked.

"Yes, surely," cried Paddy.

Pearl gave them a funny look, as if to say, 'not so funny'.

Night fell, and Blue did not appear. He did not arrive the following day, nor the one after that, though Pearl kept watch. The pigeons wondered where he was. He was such a strong flyer – maybe a falcon had killed him? Had he got lost, or too tired to fly home? The mystery tormented them. It was also a lesson, a reminder that this flying business was serious. Definitely not a holiday camp, just as Sergeant Drew had said.

10

The big test was soon to come. It made the fifty-mile drop look like a teddy bear's picnic.

That day, Sergeant McLean came into the loft at dawn. He chose the four fastest pigeons – Paddy, Snow-Girl, Anji and Bouncer – and bustled them into two wooden boxes. In they went, two per box, placed beak-to-tail and separated by a wooden partition. It was cramped, but the boxes had windows at the front, permitting the birds to look out.

Sergeant McLean gave them a light breakfast. Then he took them out into the cool morning to a waiting jeep. They were off on a journey, destination unknown.

Within an hour, the jeep stopped. Lifting the two boxes, the loftman walked to an old stone pier. Peeping from their windows, the pigeons saw fishing boats like the ones that used to jostle in Carnlough Harbour. However, this sea looked bigger than the one at home and more frightening somehow.

"Here they are," Sergeant McLean said to a man standing by a fishing trawler. They shared a joke – something about whiskey – and Sergeant McLean handed over the pigeons. He returned to the jeep, without looking back.

The pigeons were shocked. This new person brought them down some steep steps into a tiny kitchen – known in sailor-speak as a 'galley'. He stacked them on a shelf with a high rim, and he disappeared as well. A sudden throb, and an engine kicked into life. The pigeons were on their own.

It took time for their nerves to settle. The monotonous hum of the engine helped, and there were plenty of new sights for curious young pigeons. Spray frothed against the porthole in the galley wall and seagulls soared by, crying for fish. Someone whistled up on deck, happy to be at sea on a sunny, if windy, summer's day.

On and on the boat chugged, tilting through the water. The green-grey sea surged on the horizon, and the pigeons dozed. At last, another man arrived. Rustling in a bag, he gave them some seed and prepared a meal for his crewmates. Soon the galley was full of their booming voices.

After a few minutes of banter, something became clear. This trawler was heading for a Scottish port nearly eighty miles away, but it was not looking for fish. It had secret supplies on board for an RAF station in Scotland.

The crew were slurping their tea when the Captain came in. He was the man who had taken the pigeons from Sergeant McLean. He muttered something about the radio, and had a worried look.

"And there's a storm brewing," he added. "It's looking bad." No sooner had he spoken, the boat lurched suddenly and a mug of tea crashed to the floor.

Exchanging glances, the men went back to work. The galley seemed darker and colder without them. Waves began striking the porthole savagely, as if to punish it. The seagulls vanished and the whistling up on deck also stopped. "Why can't we go back?" whispered Paddy, sensing danger. They were clearly heading into the grip of a vicious storm.

The trawler's gentle rocking turned into sickening jolts. She rose gamely with each wave-crest, plunging over the top and down again with ugly force. With each drop, the boxes jumped on the shelf, smacking the pigeons' skulls against the roof of their wooden containers. Only the shelf's rim kept the birds from crashing to the floor.

Paddy hunched miserably. His head was battered, his feathers damp and ruffled. This crashing motion was merciless, like a fair-ground ride that would not stop.

The pigeons slept again. The boat's jolting had worsened, but the birds were too tired to stay awake.

It was dark in the galley when the pigeons woke to shouts and banging noises.

"ENGINE'S FAILED, SIR!" a man roared.

The engine coughed and spluttered, but would not start. As the boat lost power, it turned port side*. Without warning, a wall of water rose over the deck. It gushed down the steps, frothing into the galley and the engine room. Another wave followed, and the icy sea-water rose quickly. The boat tilted dangerously to one side.

"WE'RE IN TROUBLE SIR," a voice cried.

"WHAT'S OUR POSITION?" yelled the Captain. "IT'S TIME TO GET HELP."

"That's obvious!" Bouncer wise-cracked from his box. "Could have told him that ages ago."

The other pigeons guffawed, despite their misery. No matter how bad the situation, Bouncer always managed a joke.

The Captain barged into the galley. With a sudden shock the pigeons realised that *they* were part of the rescue plan. Surely not flying for help? 'I feel like a drowned rat, not a racing pigeon,' thought Paddy.

They had no choice. The Captain fumbled with the catch on each box, and another man rushed forward with four tiny strips of paper. Despite the boat's wild bucking, the men managed to roll up each strip and slip it into a plastic message-holder. Next, they fastened each container to a

* To the left

42

bird's leg. This was the message the pigeons had to bring to RAF Ballykelly. If they failed, the trawler's crew might drown or be wiped out by a cruising German U-boat.

The Captain struggled up the stairs, thumping the boxes on each step as he went. "I never thought I'd have to use these birds on their first day!" he muttered. Up on deck, he wedged himself in the door-frame. Opening the metal clasps on the door of each box, the man steadied himself. A brief pause, then he tossed the pigeons one by one, high into the biting wind.

Paddy and his three friends battled skywards. Below them, the sea rose and fell like a white-horned monster. Rain clouds were bearing down, but the pigeons could see the sharp black rocks of Ailsa Craig rising from the sea. The boat and its crew were in serious trouble...

The pigeons pushed up, up, away from the treacherous waves and set their sights on the horizon. Somehow they

knew the way home. The biggest danger was getting too wet – or too tired – to continue. They flew on doggedly, driven by instinct and their good training. On and on, in a tight group, without any mischief. Rain stabbed their bodies, but they continued their strong, steady strokes. At last, the wind dropped to a breeze and the storm clouds shrank to the horizon. A pale moon gleamed on the sea, and the rain eased to a drizzle.

A few miles from land, a flock of herring gulls chorused a greeting. "*Kee-yow-yow-yow*," they called. A handful of gulls joined them in flight. 'Danger!' thought Paddy, but these gulls were just curious, and had no wish to mob them. The pigeons reached the shore-line. More rocks loomed ahead, cut into strange black columns that resembled a series of stepping-stones. The Giant's Causeway!

They followed the coast. Over the harbours of Portrush and Portstewart, then a curved beach just before RAF Ballykelly. Before long, the pigeons were circling the base. Stretching their tired wings, and fanning out their tail feathers, they dropped onto the loft's landing board.

Sergeant McLean came running towards them. He had heard the reports of a serious storm in the North Channel, and was keeping an eye out for his pigeons.

"Well done, laddies!" he exclaimed as he rattled a seed can in greeting. The pigeons needed no encouragement. They slipped through the bars of the loft and let him snap open their message containers. Each bird was carrying the same vital note:

"S.O.S. Trawler Venus. Ex-Portstewart, Northern Ireland. Taking water. Position 5517N, 00506W near Ailsa Craig, off Scotland. 20.45 hrs. Send lifeboat now!"

11

Thanks to the Carnlough pigeons, the crew was rescued. Even the gruff Sergeant Drew was pleased. A reporter from a local newspaper interviewed Sergeant McLean and took a photo in the loft. 'Winged Heroes', the article called them. It told how they had raced over towering seas, infested with German U-boats, to save the five brave fishermen. The trawler's real mission was not mentioned.

"To think that was us," Snow-Girl cooed. She puffed up her chest. "I wonder does Mr. Hughes know?"

He certainly did. That Sunday, he and Annie went to Angela's house for lunch. As they sat down to their soup, Tommy quizzed him (as he did every time they met): "Any news of Paddy and the others, Uncle Andrew?"

Mr. Hughes opened his wallet and handed him the newspaper cutting, which he had folded into a small square. He gave the others a sly wink, and said not a word.

"There's Paddy, Snow-Girl, Bouncer and Anji, Ma!" shrieked Tommy, recognising the pigeons instantly. "They're after saving men's lives at sea." He began reading bits of the article out loud. "From a boat. In a storm. German submarines everywhere, and twenty-foot waves. Imagine!"

"You said they were good pigeons, Andrew," Annie said proudly.

"Aye, and it won't be the last we hear from them," he replied. "Mark my words."

*   *   *

Back at RAF Ballykelly, Sergeant McLean now chose these pigeons for the toughest jobs. When a boat or seaplane had to cross the North Channel, and the forecast was bad, he relied on them. The Moyleen Loft pigeons always homed swiftly, not a feather out of place. But they rarely arrived in a tight group any more. Some found poor weather conditions, like heavy rain or sea-fog, very tiring. Paddy was stronger, and often homed long before the others.

He was a yearling now, white with grizzled-black feathers on his neck, wings and back. Powerfully built, he had the stamina of a pigeon twice his size.

One day, in early March 1944, Sergeant McLean got an unexpected phone call.

"Sergeant Drew here," the voice went.

"What's the news?" Sergeant McLean replied.

"RAF Ballykelly is shutting down its pigeon Air/Sea Rescue service. Part of a re-organisation of the NPS. It's happening at other RAF stations as well," Sergeant Drew said breezily. "Most pigeons will return to their breeders' lofts, but a few are needed in England – for Special Operations."

"Special Operations?" said a surprised Sergeant McLean.

"Yes, work with the French Resistance, things like that. We'd like you to go to England, and bring a few of your best pigeons with you," Sergeant Drew continued. "Be ready on Monday, won't you?"

With that, the phone clicked dead.

Two days later, Paddy and Bouncer boarded an RAF plane with their trainer. It was hard to leave the flock, but Paddy and Bouncer were secretly proud. Sergeant McLean said that only the very best pigeons were picked for RAF service in England. They were the chosen ones.

On this occasion, they shared their lightweight travel

basket with eight other birds from RAF stations across Northern Ireland. This was the cream of the RAF pigeon corps in Ulster. Sergeant McLean strapped the basket into a window seat at the rear of the plane. After take-off, the pigeons muscled for a better view.

"Watch it!" Bouncer growled, caught in a rugby scrum for a glimpse of the Irish Sea.

Paddy was cool and detached, as usual. While most pigeons scrabbled and trod on each others' backs, he was calm. He gazed around him nonchalantly.

'You wouldn't know it, but he's probably the toughest pigeon on board,' Bouncer mused.

As the plane roared towards its destination, even Paddy got excited. The aircraft turned sharply, giving the pigeons a full view of creamy cliffs, topped with green. Further down the coast, they saw sandy beaches covered with coils of barbed wire and other strange objects.

"Someone's made a dog's dinner of that beach," observed Bouncer.

"I'd say they want to keep people away," said Paddy.

The plane approached a runway. They seemed to be in a military base, twice the size of RAF Ballykelly, with even higher fences and large flat-roofed buildings for storing planes. As the wheels struck the ground and the engines screamed towards shutdown, Paddy felt a tickling sense of expectation.

'Here we go again,' he thought.

12

Their new home was RAF Hurn, set in rolling countryside a few miles from the coastal town of Bournemouth. The loft was clean, simple – and crammed with pigeons. That evening, Sergeant McLean came to feed them himself with a treat of fine bird seed. They clamoured at his feet, pecking his boots mischievously.

"Now there, laddies," he laughed. "You're rarin' to go!"

After supper, the pigeons jostled to claim new perches. Paddy found himself next to a lovely white hen. Snow-Girl was a pretty pigeon, but this one was special. Earlier on, some cocks had tried to impress her, puffing up their neck feathers and fanning their tails as they strutted to and fro. They also chased her around the loft, to her disgust. She was on her own now, so Paddy decided to introduce himself.

Fluffing up his feathers, he cooed gently. The hen tilted her head. He hopped into her nesting box and paced in a tight circle, repeating his soft cooing call. She pecked some corn, pretending to be busy. But she raised her head, drawn to this unusual black-and-white stranger. Presently, she did her own little dance.

Her name was Princess, and she came from a family of champion racing pigeons in Devon.

That evening, Paddy and Princess cooed incessantly to each other. Paddy also fed her corn from his beak, which she graciously accepted. All around, pigeons were making special friends, including Bouncer. He had met a girl pigeon called Tweak, who had pale grey feathers and a dark collar.

They were getting on like a house on fire.

Some strange things happened that night. From the corner, at the base of the wooden wall, them could hear a persistent grinding noise. This went on for at least an hour. Much later, an ear-splitting siren jolted them from sleep. Outside, flashing lights lit up the night sky, revolving like powerful torches. This was followed by the *ack-ack* of gunfire from the base.

"What's that?" one pigeon called. Others repeated the same question, more sleepily.

Then, being pigeons, they dozed off again.

Many nights were disturbed like this, but the pigeons stopped paying any heed. They were locked up again to be resettled, and were busy making nests.

Paddy and Princess used bits of straw and paper to make theirs. After ten days, she laid a perfect cream egg, followed by a second, a day later. Bouncer and his mate also had two eggs in their nest box, like most of the other paired pigeons. This was part of the RAF's plan. March was the breeding season, and new chicks were urgently needed for the National Pigeon Service.

There was another good reason to let the birds pair up. When serious training started, any pigeon who was tossed hundreds of miles away would fly like a demon to return to his or her partner and their squeakers.

One evening, Princess was sitting on the eggs when she felt a tap, tap beneath her. Stepping aside, she peered into the nest. A faint crack zig-zagged across the first-laid egg. A few more taps, and a little beak appeared through a hole in the shell. The beak tapped again, at another point along the girth of the egg. It was as if the baby squeaker was rotating inside, picking places to strike in order to break the egg in half.

Princess wanted to help, but held back. The chick had to be strong enough to get out herself.

At last, a tiny leg thrust out of the egg and split it open. A wet, tired little squeaker rolled out. She flopped onto the ground and fell asleep. The second egg chipped open a few hours later, and a baby brother joined the nest.

Paddy helped feed the new chicks, just as he had shared the job of keeping the eggs warm. He was tender with his two bumbling babies.

"They're beautiful, just like you, Princess," he cooed one evening, as they stared at the two odd-looking squeakers. Jimmy and Jo had huge beaks and bodies, and skinny legs, like all ten-day-old pigeons. Both had sprouted feathers, but they looked more like pin-cushions than baby birds.

"Thank you, Paddy," trilled Princess, who was as elegant as a lady's silk scarf.

That night, both adult birds slept soundly as the moon lit up RAF Hurn. All around, pigeons were tucked into their nest boxes, without a care in the world, until a strange sound broke the silence. Not the grinding noise from the corner, or a screaming siren. Just the thud of an object hitting the floor, followed by a high-pitched squeak and a weak beating of wings against the wall.

Paddy's eyes blinked open. He and a handful of birds began milling through the air. Some just flew in panic. Paddy zoomed to the floor of the loft to investigate as a mother pigeon cried: "My chick! My chick has fallen!"

To make matters worse, a rat was tugging her unfortunate squeaker towards a freshly-gnawed hole in the corner. The rodent had broken into the loft after nights of patient gnawing, and was delighted when this tasty 'dinner' had dropped on the straw beside him. The pigeons

had other ideas. Furious, they started to dive-bomb the invader.

"Get him, get him!" one of them shrieked. The air filled with loose feathers and floating tassels of straw as pigeons crashed into the wall. Two landed on the rat's sinewy back. He reared up on his hind legs, hissing angrily. But, he released the chick and slithered into the hole.

The next morning, Sergeant McLean found the terrified squeaker on the ground. Though cold and limp with shock, the youngster had only lost a few feathers. Sergeant McLean gave him a sugar-and-water drink and popped him back into his parents' nest. Another man came and nailed a chunk of wood over the hole the rat had made. It had strips of metal to stop the rat, or any of his family, from breaking into the loft again.

"That'll keep the boyo out," Bouncer kept saying. "A close shave! A close shave!"

13

By late March, 1944, the pigeons were resettled in their new loft. It was time to start work.

Sergeant McLean, having been made chief loftman at RAF Hurn, was in charge of training. He took his job very seriously, and knew his RAF pigeon training manual by heart. This manual was the loftman's bible, used to prepare thousands of birds in the National Pigeon Service for their role as messengers in the war.

The manual advised a gentle start to training. Once the pigeons were resettled, Sergeant McLean simply released them outside the loft so they could fly back in. He rewarded them immediately with seed, just as Mr. Hughes had done. This lesson learned, the pigeons could be released to stretch their wings and explore RAF Hurn.

The ideal time was before supper. On the first evening, Sergeant McLean quietly opened the trap in front of the loft. Sun-lit air surged into the musty room, laced with smells of aviation fuel and freshly-cut grass. One by one, the pigeons fluttered to the entrance and stepped onto the landing board. With a powerful whirring of wings, they shot into the sky.

"Free-ee…" called Paddy.

"Whee-ee…" his brother replied.

They soared in ever-changing circles, twisting over stubby green planes, sprawling hangars and the tall wire fences that separated RAF Hurn from the outside world. After a few laps, it was time for a new game. At a secret signal, the flock rose in a tall wave and climbed hundreds of feet, before sweeping back to the ground. It felt scary, but delicious.

After twenty minutes, Sergeant McLean rattled the feed can. The pigeons dropped obediently into their loft.

"Well done, laddies. Well done!" their trainer said. He stroked each pigeon in turn, just as Mr. Hughes used to do, clearly delighted.

There were around 200 pigeons at RAF Hurn, divided among different lofts. Sergeant McLean needed a helper. Private Mike was a farmer's son from Wales, just a few years older than Tommy in Carnlough. His quiet lilting voice reminded the birds of their real home, in Northern Ireland. The pigeons respected Sergeant McLean, but there was something special about Mike. He had a thin, hungry-looking face and a quiet way about him. Mike loved pigeons, and he never rushed them.

"Ea-sy. Ea-sy," he used to say, if the birds got fussed. Sometimes, when he was alone in the loft, he would dip into his pocket and pull out a shiny metal object. Puffing with his mouth, he could create strange tunes from this thing, making the very air dance.

Guided by Sergeant McLean, he fed the pigeons an ever-changing mixture of yellow corn (maize), seeds, dry beans and peas. There was always a bowl of grit, to help them digest their food, and plenty of fresh water. Every week, the two men checked each pigeon for signs of sickness and injury. They wanted the birds in peak condition.

Then Sergeant McLean began choosing birds for short and long 'drops' away from the loft. The weather was glorious and the pigeons homed like clockwork from 15-mile and 20-mile liberation points. Sergeant McLean wrote all their times in a little black notebook just as he had done in RAF Ballykelly.

He seemed particularly pleased with Paddy. When visitors came to the loft, he would point to his black-and-white 'student,' perched in the nest box with Princess and the two squeakers, Jimmy and Jo. "A most intelligent pigeon," he would say. "And very fast, too."

Sergeant McLean never failed to recount the story of the boat rescue in Northern Ireland, always with juicy new details added in. The visitors would stand stiffly in their clean clothes, trying to avoid pigeon droppings on the floor. But the story of Paddy and Bouncer always impressed them.

One day, a man arrived at the loft in a smart uniform, with black shoes so shiny you could see your reflection in them. A young girl and boy came with him – the little lad clinging fiercely to his father's leg. Sergeant McLean caught Paddy and held him, so the children could stroke his feathers. Then he lifted each child, so they could peek into the nest to see Jimmy and Jo. The little boy beamed, forgetting his shyness.

"Daddy! Daddy! He's a lovely pigeon," the girl cried.

"One of my best," Sergeant McLean said, giving their father a meaningful look. "Very fast. A *most* intelligent pigeon."

"Good. Try him out solo this week – see how he does," the man replied quietly. "We only want the cream of this bunch for the French operation. And use one of those new message containers, won't you? We've had problems with the metal ones."

Sergeant McLean nodded. With that, Sergeant McLean and the man left, the children skipping at their heels.

"He's top brass, him," Mike whispered to the pigeons.

"The boys on the base are all talking about this France business. That man knows all about it, I'm sure."

Everyone knew RAF Hurn was gearing up for something big, but nobody knew quite what. In the past week, planes had taken off from the base nearly every night, droning down the runway under a cloak of darkness. Their targets were bridges, railways and roads in Northern France – destroying these communication lines made it harder for the Germans to move around. By day, the base rang to the sound of marching boots and roared commands:

"LEFT! RIGHT! LEFT! RIGHT!"

"ABOUT TURN!"

"ATTENTION!!!!"

One afternoon, Sergeant McLean and Mike arrived in the loft together, looking very business-like. The pigeons shuffled nervously in their nest boxes, sensing that something was about to happen.

Mike swiftly caught Paddy, and Sergeant McLean fixed a green plastic container to the pigeon's leg. To his horror, they locked him in a wooden carrier box, without so much as a grain of corn to nibble. Hours dragged by, with Paddy hunched stiffly in his prison on the loft floor. Mike returned to feed the others, but not Paddy. At last Sergeant McLean reappeared. Scooping up Paddy's container, he spoke briefly to Mike. Without further ado, he walked smartly to an army jeep with Paddy. They sped out of RAF Hurn on another unknown mission.

'Here we go again,' Paddy thought.

They drove for a long, long time. Paddy felt miserable in the cramped box, but he was also afraid of being released on his own. Thoughts of Princess, the chicks and a tasty bowl of corn flitted through his brain. At last, the jeep pulled up.

They were by a gate, leading into a quiet field. Dusk had fallen; the air was cool and foggy. At least there were no boats, though Paddy could detect a hint of saltiness in the breeze.

"Now, my boy," Sergeant McLean said. "Time for you to get flying. Sorry about the supper – a pigeon can't fly on a full stomach…!"

The man unclipped the box. Holding Paddy in two strong hands, he tossed the bird high into the air.

'Where am I?' was Paddy's first thought, as he shot skyward with a whirring of wings.

Soon it would be dark. Paddy had flown at night-time and in storms, but never in fog. At first, he circled high above the ground. Scanning below, he saw the vague outline of fields and the road he must have taken with Sergeant McLean. He followed it. A few wing-beats later he was flying over a town. The air grew warmer and the fog thinned. Rows and rows of houses were now visible, spreading beneath him. The town was blacked-out, but Paddy could see shirts flapping on clothes lines and chimneys poking from dark-slated roofs.

Small roads connected all these houses to each other. They linked into a bigger road, which ran beside the dark glinting sea on his left. RAF Hurn was near the sea, due west from this place… Paddy suddenly had a flash of understanding – a sort of pigeon brain-wave. This big road would bring him home.

Darkness or not, Paddy could read a landscape like a book. He flew confidently, enjoying the damp summer night and the solitude. The fog was not a problem. He flew as fast as he could, home to Princess and the squeakers.

Zooming inland, he came upon a great forest which stretched as far as he could see. Under the half moon, Paddy saw strange glints coming from the trees, and sections where the forest had been cut away by men and machines. He slowed, taking a closer look. Under the thick forest canopy were dozens of trucks, like the ones from RAF Hurn, and guns mounted on wheels.

Paddy was tired. He landed on a pine tree. Glancing down, he spotted a square-shaped 'mound' tucked between the trees. It looked like a stack of boxes covered by a dark cloth. Other strange 'mounds' jutted up ahead, each hidden from prying eyes.

'What are they?' Paddy wondered. He darted his head nervously, to gaze at his surroundings. This place was scary. Shadows moved, and the trees rustled and squeaked as if they were full of wild animals. At last, he managed to shut his eyes and nap.

"*KEE-AW!*" burst a blood-curdling shriek a tree-top away. Paddy rose in a panic, nearly jumping out of his feathers. Was it a falcon…? No. Instead, a ghostly bird swooped by, its face as pale and round as the moon, with staring eyes. It was an owl, looking for mice – not pigeons. But Paddy was too skittish to stay.

'Time to go,' he thought. He lifted into the air and flew as fast as his wings would take him.

The mystery of the hidden trucks and guns deepened a mile later. At the edge of the forest was a newly-built gravel road. It was partly hidden with large branches and grass cuttings. The people who had made this road did not want it to be discovered. Perhaps they were hiding all those tanks and boxes from someone? Why?

Paddy flew on, the light now stronger. He crossed a small valley that cut straight to the sea. Here he spotted train engines, stacked on lorries with gigantic flat-bottomed trailers. The trains were partly covered by the same cloth that he had seen in the forest. It was a strange place to hide so many trains. But then, he had seen many odd things tonight.

14

Wheeling above Hurn village at dawn, Paddy skimmed the little cottages and the wood-cutter's yard just as rosy light warmed the sky. He banked neatly over the air-base, and glided straight to his loft.

'Home,' thought Paddy as he touched the landing board. He was eager to see his family, and he was ravenous. Mike was on dawn watch, ready with breakfast and a smile. Moments later, Paddy was gulping down corn and cool draughts of water. Then he fell into a relaxing sleep.

Rest was a luxury in the weeks that followed. Soldiers and pigeons alike trained constantly, to be as fit and ready as possible. For what, they still did not know.

Every day, men paraded in the base, and lined up in columns with great packs on their shoulders. Sometimes they did strange exercises, stretching their arms and legs, as other men shouted at them. One wet evening, on a fly-about, the pigeons saw Mike returning to the base with a group of soldiers. They had just completed a gruelling march through the New Forest. All the men had streaky black faces, and looked exhausted.

It was a Friday night, so despite his tiredness Mike went off to the village pub. The next morning, he was his usual sprightly self and bursting with news.

"There's Yanks* in the village now! O boys!" he chanted as he tipped corn into the pigeons' food trays. "They were in the pub last night. Dressed all fancy, and drinking beer. They

* Americans

had loads of chocolate bars and chewing gum. Delicious…And guide-books for Great Britain, as well. Imagine that. *Guide-books*!!!"

Mike chuckled, but his face grew serious. "Some of these Yanks will be working on the base with us. They're off to France as well. I suppose our RAF lads will be too. Well, there's plenty for me to do today – I'll see you boys." He left the loft.

That afternoon, trucks revved into RAF Hurn, laden with rolls of barbed wire and fence posts. Teams of men strung this deadly wire on the perimeter fence, with much hammering and yells. When the work was done, officers posted armed sentries along the wire. From now on, Mike and his friends would not be allowed to leave RAF Hurn. Even the villagers were not allowed to visit. The camp was sealed.

Sergeant McLean ate his supper in a crowded mess hall that night. He was deep in thought when he felt a tap on his shoulder. It was the Camp Commandant, no less. Sergeant McLean rose to his feet, saluting hastily.

"At ease, Sergeant," the man said. "The senior officers have a briefing this evening. At 20.00 hours. In the big marquee." He looked the loftman square in the eye. "Very important. Be there, won't you?"

"Yes, *SIR!!*" Sergeant McLean replied.

The Commandant swung on his heels and left.

Sergeant McLean gasped when he walked into the briefing tent at 8 o'clock hours sharp. A vast model made of sand, earth, crinkly paper and other bits and pieces lay on a long trestle table. Expertly constructed, it had a strip of vivid blue sea with coastline on either side. Real sand had been used to make the beaches, and there were even toy boats on the water. Inland, there were towns, bridges, roads and railway stations. The model was pin-pricked with little red flags; some had pictures of guns on them.

A giant map hung from the wall of the tent. RAF Hurn and other RAF stations along the south coast of England had been marked in. Thick black arrows pointed across the English Channel to a series of beaches on the French coast. It looked like Normandy, but Sergeant McLean was not sure, as he had never been to France. Dominating the map, he saw the words:

OPERATION OVERLORD

15

The briefing was about to commence. Sergeant McLean slipped into a seat as an officer strode towards the map. This man was tall, solidly-built and wore a gaze that simply commanded respect. Silence fell. He began to speak, very deliberately.

"Welcome, officers. The day that we have all been preparing for has almost arrived. The Supreme Headquarters Allied Expeditionary Force – SHAEF, as you know – headed by the Supreme Commander, Dwight Eisenhower, has spent a year planning an Allied invasion of France. What I am about to tell you is still 'Top Secret'. I needn't say anymore on that point…" He paused.

Sergeant McLean tilted forward in his seat, listening intently. The atmosphere in the marquee was electric.

"The invasion is code-named Operation Overlord, as you can see. An estimated 130,000 men will cross the English Channel, in a flotilla of vessels over 4,000-strong, from these various ports, under cover of dark. They will rendezvous by the Isle of Wight – here – and proceed to the Normandy coast. Warships will attack enemy positions first, and our men will disembark at dawn on D-Day. They will storm the beaches on a low, incoming tide."

He took up a long, metal-tipped stick.

"Here we have the five beaches: SWORD, JUNO, GOLD, OMAHA and UTAH," he continued, striking each location on the map, one after the other. His stick made a pinging sound that shot through the room. 'Like tiny bullets,' Sergeant McLean thought.

"Our job in the RAF is three-fold," the officer continued. "The night before D-Day, British and US airborne divisions will drop thousands of men, by glider and parachute, inland from these five designated beaches – chiefly here." He struck the map again. "Their main task is to destroy bridges, cut telephone wires and attack enemy gun batteries that could inflict a lot of damage on our troops.

"Bomber pilots will follow, targeting key communication points later in the night, and gun batteries in the morning. Our boys from RAF Hurn may be among them – I can't say at this stage. Thirdly, our coastal-based bombers will be on call to protect the vessels involved in Operation Overlord." He paused again, calmly scanning the intent faces of the men. "Any questions?"

"When is D-Day, Sir?" someone behind Sergeant McLean asked.

"That's still classified information, I'm afraid. The optimum conditions – a full moon and low, rising tide – occur in early June. The actual date will be dictated by weather conditions closer to the time, but we're probably looking at June 5th."

Sergeant McLean felt a rush of excitement mingled with fear. Images of grey, heaving seas flashed through his mind. He saw landing craft full of men, ploughing towards gun-strafed beaches... and the unknown. He thought of his sister's young lad, Jimmy, who had enlisted just a few months ago. 'Only eighteen, and he'll be heading into this,' Sergeant McLean thought grimly.

Other officers quizzed the speaker about the weather, planning, supplies – important matters. He gave all the information he could, promising to follow up with detailed operational plans. Sergeant McLean wanted to ask if the pigeons were needed, but it seemed too trivial somehow.

"Ah, I almost forgot," the speaker added. "Sergeant McLean."

"Sir?"

"We have a job for you – and your feathered friends. Clear, accurate communications will be vital to the success of Operation Overlord and the D-Day landings. Radios can get jammed, as you know, and signals can be intercepted. We must know how our boys are doing on D-Day and where reinforcements are needed."

"Yes, Sir," Sergeant McLean replied, conscious that several officers were staring at him in surprise. Others were openly smiling.

"The US First Army has requested RAF Hurn and other air-bases to release pigeons to various operational units as part of the invasion plans. The pigeons must be delivered to the Americans in baskets, with food and water for up to five days. They will travel to Normandy with the D-Day troops, or as required, and must be liberated within four or five days. You should pick the best pigeons, prepare your equipment – message containers, all that – and await further instructions. Understood?"

"They'll be ready, Sir," Sergeant McLean said.

His head was buzzing as he left the marquee. This was a big job. He and Mike had to get it right.

16

Late May, 1944. RAF Hurn's runways shook beneath the wheels of departing RAF planes at night, and visiting US bombers by day. More trucks and jeeps sped into the base, laden with supplies and equipment. Much of this material had been hidden in the New Forest and other secret locations until now, waiting for a vast assembly line that would carry it to the beaches of Normandy on D-Day.

Across England, thousands of soldiers were on the move, packed in trains and truck convoys that rolled nose-to-tail, down track and road. They were heading for sealed 'transit' camps near the south coast. There they would wait for the ships, planes and gliders that would bring them to Normandy.

Sergeant McLean still had not received instructions from the National Pigeon Service, or from his Air Ministry contact in Adastral House, London. He decided to choose fifty of his best pigeons for Operation Overlord; a mixture of yearlings and mature birds, cocks and hens. He scrutinised each bird thoroughly, checking its homing records in his little black book. Next came a physical examination: a careful check of the eyes, throat, wing feathers, and leg ring. He even inspected each pigeon's droppings for signs of disease, as he had got a worrying report about canker from the head loftman at the pigeon loft in Fort Widley, near Portsmouth.

At Sergeant McLean's bidding, Mike spent a lot of time in the lofts, talking to his 'boyos' in a reassuring sing-song voice. "Pity I won't be making the journey with you," he told them. "The US Army has a special job for you boyos. Top Secret! Top Secret!"

Paddy and Bouncer swelled with pride. A few pigeons from the next door loft had already been on special missions to France. Some had even dropped by parachute, with a secret agent, deep into the French countryside. The agent's job was to get scraps of information about German troops from people who were working for the French Resistance. The agent had to write a coded message, and tuck it into the pigeon's message container. The bird's job was to bring it back to RAF Hurn.

That was important work, but Operation Overlord sounded much better.

So when would it start? The talk was June 5th, until the bad weather started rattling everyone's nerves. Late May had been glorious, but the fine spell broke on the first Friday in June. That weekend dragged. The pigeons, imprisoned in the loft, grew tense and bored. Sergeant McLean had stopped the distance training. A short evening excursion around the base was all he permitted his birds.

Sunday, June 4th arrived – with miserable weather. The loft hatch remained firmly shut. There was no evening fly-about, but at least Mike had some news. "Not tonight, boyos," he announced. "They say the forecast is too bad for the ships to go to France. Massive waves," he said, rolling his arms in the air. "Storms. Looks like we might be leaving tomorrow instead. They say D-Day may be June 6th. Depends on the weather."

After spilling corn into the metal trays, Mike seemed in no hurry to leave. Instead, he fished the harmonica from his pocket, and sat on the floor. As the pigeons gobbled their corn, he squeezed out a sweet lilting tune. To their delight, he played song after song on his silver instrument. That night, lightning cracked the sky and torrential rain beat like a thousand drums on the huts of RAF Hurn. Yet the loft remained calm.

17

Monday June 5th brought cool blustery weather, and even more activity on the base. Airmen lined up their packs near the main runway, and moved supplies this way and that. Others tinkered with planes. Late in the day, an officer found paint in the hangar. The men sloshed it under the wings and body of the aircraft until the planes glistened with black-and-white stripes.

Before tea, Mike released the pigeons for a brief fly-about. After looping the base in great figures of eight, the pigeons flurried onto the loft's roof. The sun shone fiercely through a gap in a heavily clouded sky, scorching their backs. Soldiers lolled on the grass below, scribbling letters and playing card games. A few men kicked a football, thudding it into the perimeter fence.

"G'wan will ye!" one lanky player said, in a voice that reminded them of their home in Carnlough. "My granny can kick better than that!"

"Get out of it!" his mate replied.

Si-si-si-si-si came the thin rattle of the seed can from inside the loft. Mike had arrived.

"Aha, supper," said Paddy, quickly losing interest in the football.

"Could be our last!" Bouncer wise-cracked.

After their feed, the pigeons crouched in their nest boxes. They strained to hear the door open, or planes leaving the base, but all was strangely quiet. Chicks bumbled around the loft, annoying the older birds. Darkness closed in. Still no sign of a travel basket, or any news.

D-Day was definitely tomorrow, Tuesday June 6th, 1944, because Mike had said so. But for now, neither pigeons nor bomber planes from RAF Hurn were going anywhere.

*   *   *

Outside RAF Hurn, an awesome drama had been unfolding across the southern tip of England since dawn.

Army trucks full of British, American and Canadian troops had sped through sleepy little hamlets like Hurn, heading for Portsmouth, Southampton and other departure points. Groups of adults and children cheered the brave soldiers as they passed by, waving flags and handkerchiefs. But some women cried, thinking of their own husbands and sons.

Down at the docks, the trucks disgorged a human cargo – and what a sight the docks were! Boats of every conceivable shape and size were waiting for the troops, tightly moored but pointing towards France, ready to go.

Proudest of all were the battleships and cruisers, standing majestic by the quaysides. Packed around them were cargo boats and supply ships, tugs and destroyers. Low in the water, like hundreds of metal crabs, were Landing Craft, Tanks (LCTs). Their job was to ferry small numbers of specially waterproofed tanks to within yards of the Normandy beaches, then unload them.

Navy ships were moored outside the harbours, standing guard. Scruffy little fishing boats bobbed in every spare mooring.

Vast balloons swung from the bigger vessels, suspended by steel cables as thick as a man's arm. They looked like decorations at a giant's birthday party, but in fact they were barrage balloons filled with explosive hydrogen gas and festooned with nets. Any German plane that dived to attack a ship would do so at its peril.

Men swarmed onto their designated craft, bent under the weight of their packs. Officers barked orders as cranes hoisted crates off the docks and into the holds of waiting ships. At times, the cargo swung just over the soldiers' heads, prompting roars of "Eh! Watch it, mate!"

Some men had been living on the battleships for several days, and were bored. They hung over the railings, smoking cigarettes and swapping stories. When marching music suddenly burst from a loud-hailer on the battleships, they cheered.

From 12.00 hours, ships began streaming out of the harbours to a meeting point just off the Isle of Wight, code-named 'Piccadilly Circus'. The sea was choppy, the wind knifingly cold. The troops sat down to splendid feasts of steak or chicken, mashed potatoes and frozen peas, followed by ice cream or canned fruit salad. Within a few hours, some men felt so sick they regretted every single mouthful.

At 18.30 hours, the BBC broadcast a long-awaited signal to the French Resistance fighters, who listened secretly in their cellars and outhouses:

"It is hot in Suez. It is hot in Suez," the message began. It repeated those words, then silence fell. The announcer continued: *"The dice are on the carpet. The dice are on the carpet."*

The coded message meant only one thing: D-Day was imminent.

At dusk, Spitfire planes patrolled leaden skies over the English Channel to ward off any attackers.

At 22.30 hours, an almighty roar rent the air. Planes began

thundering over the vast flotilla of boats which was now heaving its way through the sea to Normandy. Each plane towed a glider, crammed with soldiers and equipment. Like the bombers, these Horsa gliders had black-and-white stripes under their wings, to reduce the risk of being hit by the 'friendly fire' of Allied guns. They looked as mysterious as swans, soaring through the darkening sky. But, like swans, they were poor fliers. Many would crash in France, splintering into a million fragments of wood, casting their crews onto the hard, unforgiving ground.

An hour later, more Dakotas* left for France, carrying men who would parachute into enemy-held territory. Their job was to attack bridges, gun positions and other targets, and help weaken the German response to the D-Day landings.

Around 24.00 hours, when the skies were totally dark, bomber pilots took off from RAF bases near the coast for a two-hour flight across the Channel. Visibility was poor, with thick cloud obscuring a full moon. The planes flew in tight V-shape formations, laden with their deadly cargo. More bombers, including three Typhoon squadrons from RAF Hurn, would set out at dawn to cast a necklace of flame on the beaches of Normandy.

At H-Hour – 06.30 hours on June 6th, 1944 – the men on the ships would plunge into the sea, and fight to liberate Europe.

Those that survived this perilous mission to France, would never, ever forget D-Day.

* A type of WW2 plane

18

June 6th at RAF Hurn passed quietly, after the bombers returned to base around 08.30 hours. The pigeons perched in the loft – waiting, waiting.

Barely fifty miles away, a young American soldier sat on his straw mattress in a transit camp, also waiting. D-Day had passed him by, too, and he was restless. He tried to write a letter home, but it was hard. The bed was as lumpy as hell and the dormitory too rowdy. Anyway, he was hardly allowed to say anything in these letters – the censor was really strict and took chunks out of everyone's mail.

"Hey, gimme a break!" Howard yelled, but his buddies ignored him.

Chewing on his pencil, he managed a few lines:

Tuesday June 6th, 1944

Dear Mom,
Thanks for the cookies. They tasted real good, and arrived pretty well in one piece. Please send more! The rations here aren't so hot — like I said, lots of tinned meat, dried eggs and potatoes and a bit of canned fruit, if you're lucky.

Still, we get seven packs of cigarettes a week (no Mom, I don't smoke, but I trade them for other rations!!) and real Hershey chocolate bars. And we eat a whole lot better than the English people. Sometimes we slip supplies to our friends' Moms, like flour and sugar, and they make us cakes. They are always grateful for anything we can give them.

I got a pass out the other night, and we went into ———— for a drink (I can't tell you where, sorry!). That was fun. We got to London a few weeks back by train, into a place called Paddington. London sure is a fine city, and the folks were real kind to us.

How's my favorite kid sister? Tell Becky I'm saving my candy bars for her and that there's a stray cat in our new camp she'd just <u>love</u>. I call him Fred — that's a real English name, isn't it? We're off on a big trip soon, but we haven't been told much so I can't say any more.

I'll write again soon.

Your loving son,
Howard

P.S. Don't forget the cookies!!!!

Howard could not tell his Mom any news about D-Day, or about this Operation Overlord business. Until a week ago, he and his fellow soldiers from the 2nd Armored Division, US First Army, had been stationed in an army barracks at Tidworth, near a town called Salisbury in southern England. Many of his older buddies had seen action in North Africa and Sicily, in 1943, but Howard had come straight from training in Fort Benning, Georgia, USA, on a rough-looking ocean liner. It had taken forever, and he had been sick as a dog most of the time.

Life had been tough at Tidworth, too. The 2nd Armored was like a miniature army, based around a tank division, and it lived up to its motto, 'Hell on Wheels'. The brass – as they called the senior officers – had wanted to land the 2nd Armored Division in France on D-Day but decided there just was not enough room on the beach for so many tanks with all those men disembarking at the same time. It would have been chaotic.

Right now, as waves of American soldiers were battling desperately on Omaha beach, the 2nd Armored Division was in a transit camp, close to its departure port. It would start arriving on Omaha Beach on D-Day + 3, that is, three days after the first Normandy landings.

"Hey, Howard. Glower wants you," shouted Rob, Howard's best buddy. "Something to do with pigeons. Beat that!"

Howard bolted upright on his mattress. He could hardly believe his ears – pigeons? His job in the 82nd Battalion was 'recce'* work, in other words, scouting and passing on information that would help the 2nd Armored's battle plans. He had a bit of French, which was why he had volunteered – and had been selected – for this battalion. So, what was this stuff about pigeons?

Sergeant Glower sat in his office, wearing a funny look.

"Sit down, Howard," he commanded. "You're a farm boy, so this job should suit you down to the ground. Know anything about pigeons?"

"Used to shoot them, Sir."

* Short for 'reconnaissance'.

"Son, you won't be doin' that this time. These are special pigeons, homin' pigeons."

"Yes, Sir," said Howard, trying not to smirk.

"Quit foolin', son," Sergeant Glower snapped. "We're taking delivery of some pigeons from a local RAF air-base on Thursday. That'll be just before we leave here to embark for France. Ya'll get a briefin' on the invasion plans this afternoon."

'That's it,' thought Howard. 'Thursday…'

"Now, your pigeons'll have food and water for five days, and you will get instructions on delivery," Sergeant Glower said. "They will be YOUR responsibility, Howard. DO YOUR JOB. Release them with any info'mation you can get, as and when you need to. Understood?"

"Yes, Sir," Howard replied, his face a mask.

When the 2nd Armored Division (AD) had been left behind on D-Day, Howard had felt strangely disappointed. Now France was just a few days away – and he had a mission, even if meant taking charge of some 'dumb' pigeons.

19

The next 48 hours passed in a blur.

Howard got his pack, which included a stock of 'funny money' for France. The guys said the notes had been printed by the Allies, but they looked real enough. More important, he had his gun, ammo, combat knife, food rations, water bottle, mess kit (to eat with), a first aid kit and some personal items. He also got his battle-gear, including a waterproof cape and a uniform that had been drenched in some chemical. It smelt foul.

That evening the soldiers lined up for a hair-cut. They had a good laugh when Rob and a few others got their heads totally shaved on either side, leaving a weird crest down the middle. It made them look like Mohican warriors, but no officers complained. Maybe they thought it would scare the enemy.

Thursday June 8th arrived with a dawn call. This was the day that the soldiers from the 2nd AD would join their landing craft for the overnight trip to France. A few men, feeling the pressure, got physically sick. Howard stayed calm.

Over in RAF Hurn, Mike was in the loft at daybreak. After consulting Sergeant McLean's notebook, he picked out thirty pigeons. He divided these among several wicker baskets, big and small, humming all the while to keep the pigeons relaxed. Down at the jeep, Sergeant McLean had the delivery list. The birds had to be brought to the US First Army that morning.

"Got the bags, Mike? And the instruction sheets?" Sergeant McLean asked.

"In the back, Sir."

"OK. Say your good-byes!"

And off they went.

*   *   *

Sergeant Glower called for Howard after breakfast. A basket made out of light brown twigs sat on his desk. Rustling noises were coming from inside.

'Hope I don't have to swim onto the beach with that,' Howard thought, trying to keep his face expressionless.

"Son, here are six pr-ize homin' pigeons," Sergeant Glower said. He held out a slip of paper. "And here's all ya need to know about lookin' after them."

Howard opened the sheet of paper. It read: TO THE ATTENTION OF PIGEON OFFICER, US FIRST ARMY, and it had headings like FEED, LIGHT, MESSAGE SENDING. Each section had carefully typed instructions. It was signed: *Sgt. McLean, Head Loftman, RAF Hurn.*

'Whoever this guy is, he knows a lot about minding pigeons,' Howard thought.

"Here's all their food, and bits and pieces," Sergeant Glower went on, nodding at a bottle-green pack propped against his desk.

Howard could not believe it. His pack already weighed a ton. How was he going to manage all this pigeon stuff? There wasn't much room in a tank, and the guys had said they might even be given push-bikes as well to take with them for scouting work in France. What a ridiculous idea. Howard sniggered again, in spite of himself.

"I've a bit of good news for ya," Glower drawled. "There's a spare Harley-Davidson motor-bike for the Unit, with a sidecar. A bit old, but the boys have kept her engine sweet. She'll go over on the LCT with the tanks. You and Corporal Green can have the bike for pigeon transport...!" He winked.

"Why, thank you, SIR!" Howard gasped. Seizing the basket, he slung the green bag over his shoulder. He was half-way to the door when he rushed back for the instruction list. Stuffing it into his pocket, he collided with the door. The pigeons were slung around in the basket, fluttering in panic.

"Where's Rob?" he roared at the first soldier he met. "Glower has given us the Harley!"

An hour later, Howard was sitting on the army truck heading towards the docks with other men from his squad. The basket was on his knee, and he saw the pigeons scrabbling inside. A white head suddenly poked out of a rectangular window cut into the front. The pigeon stared at him, blinking foolishly. Howard glared back.

"Darn thing," he said.

"He doesn't like pigeons," Paddy told Bouncer, as he pulled back into the basket.

"How come?" Bouncer replied.

"His face. It looked cross."

"He'll come round," Bouncer said confidently. "You'll see."

The pigeons' first impression of this new minder was not good, but he seemed to improve down at the docks. Howard held the basket chest-high, as he strode down the quayside with the men from his squad. Men criss-crossed the harbour, like worker ants intent on their jobs. Their group stopped by the edge of the pier. An iron ladder led to a platform below.

Moored to the platform was a cluster of compact metal boats.

"LCT 831?" called the officer from Howard's squad.

"That's right, Sir," replied a deep American voice from the platform. "We've been savin' this baby specially for you guys."

"Gee, thanks a bunch!" Rob whispered in Howard's ear. They both laughed.

One by one, the soldiers clambered onto the rectangular boat which was already loaded with tanks and trucks. Howard found a spot to stow his pack and the pigeon basket. At last they were off to Normandy. Their turn had finally come.

20

A few minutes out of the harbour, the LCT was tossing through waves like a crazy bull. The craft was uncomfortable enough, without the sea getting rough. A few soldiers got sick into paper bags. Others sat with their jaws clenched, staring.

Howard leant against the clammy steel wall of the boat, trying not to think about what lay ahead. Instead, he remembered his kid sister, Becky. How she'd love these pigeons, especially the one with the white head. Cats were Becky's favourite animal. His Mom loved cats too, but his Dad said dogs were better. 'Funny thing that, cats and dogs,' Howard mused.

Unconsciously, he touched the lucky silver dollar and chain that his parents had given him, and wished hard that he would see them again. They all had crazy rows sometimes, but his family was great. With these thoughts twirling in his head, Howard drifted into sleep.

"You done snoozin'?"

Howard sat up. It was Corporal Green, ready to brief his nine-member squad.

"We're comin' near Omaha beach real soon," the corporal shouted, hunkering down on the floor by the soldiers. His big frame filled the cramped space. "The plan is to lower the ramp of the LCT as close to the shore as we can get. We will drop our tanks into the water, and hit the beach. The good news is that there ain' no Germans on this beach any more. Now, get into your vehicles."

June 6th had brought hell to the golden sands of Omaha beach. Enemy guns had strafed the seas, cutting down men before they had even got off the ramps of their LCTs and LCIs*. The German bunkers were strung along a cliff directly overlooking the landing zone. Their guns and mortar shells had inflicted savage losses on the American troops, to the point that the US Commander General Bradley almost halted the landings on Omaha at 09.15 hours.

He had agonised, but decided to press ahead. Eventually, scores of brave soldiers from the US 2nd Ranger Battalion silenced a key battery at Pointe du Hoc, after scaling the cliffs with ropes and their bare, bloodied hands.

Today, D-Day + 3, was a different story. The DD tanks** of the 2nd Armored Division 'Hell on Wheels' paddled gently to the shore, lathered in grease, with tall snorkels fixed to their rear-ends to keep the exhaust pipe dry. There was no raking gunfire, or *Whoosh...BLAST!* of shells. Howard saw tanks and trucks lining up on the sand. Some men were working on a road leading off the beach. Others were building an artificial harbour – called a 'Mulberry' – for ships that would bring in vital supplies. The scene looked almost normal.

Until he spotted a group of men coming out of a green tent. They were bringing some poor guy on a stretcher, down to the shoreline. More wounded soldiers were carried out – one had lost a leg. A hospital ship was waiting to ferry them to England. For these soldiers, the war was over.

"K-Rations, then rest," Corporal Green announced. Howard was glad of the interruption, and he was starving.

They found a spot atop a sheltered sand dune, looking out to sea. As Howard munched his dry rations, Bouncer stuck

* Landing Craft, Infantry
** Duplex-Drive 'amphibious' Sherman tanks, that could move on water and land

out his head. He stared at the young man and his corn-coloured hair. The soldier met his gaze. Bouncer pecked the wicker-work, and shot Howard a cheeky look.

The man broke off a crust of bread and offered it to the bird. Bouncer made short work of Howard's peace offering.

"Time to feed you guys, I reckon," Howard said. Rifling through the green shoulder bag, he found the feed and water trays. He nicked open a small bag of yellow corn, marked 'Day 1', and spilled the contents into two trays which he strapped onto the basket under the holes.

It was relaxing, watching the pigeons eat. They swallowed the huge grains whole, without chewing them or anything; just opened their beaks and knocked them back. A couple of soldiers fed them bits of bread. One even tried a sliver of chocolate, until Howard stopped him.

"They ain't pets," he said. "These here are homin' pigeons. They've got to eat proper food."

He figured they were thirsty after all that dry corn, so he poured water from his canteen into the seed trays. The pigeons took turns to drink, and he spotted the one with the white head. He had black patches on his back, and looked quite handsome.

A tank started up, grinding through the sand near the soldiers. "Watch out, gentlemen," an English voice chimed.

It was time to leave Omaha beach. Corporal Green summoned the men to join their tanks and trucks. Howard stayed with Rob, the corporal and a few others in one truck. The pigeons were jammed in the back, with the soldiers' packs; the motor bike was strapped on the back. For a few heart-stopping moments, the engine strained as the wheels spun in soft sand. Then, with a rapid churning, it was off.

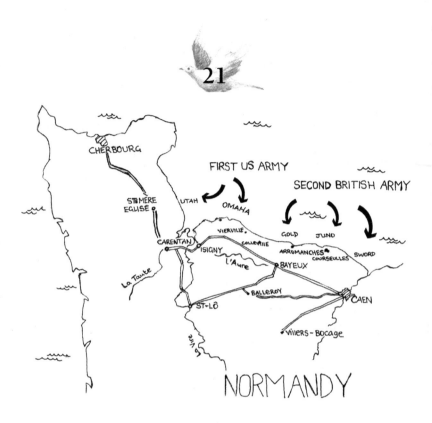

21

NORMANDY

Howard ran his finger along the map, trying to find the places that Corporal Green was hurling at him. Trevières, Isigny, Bayeux, Carentan. It was hard, because the map was hand-made and the man was really mangling the names. He was spitting out TREV-ERS, BYE-AXE and CARE-ANTAN like machine gun-fire. Howard spoke French, and those names did not sound right.

They were crouched in an apple orchard, a few miles inland from Omaha Beach. Last night, their first on French soil, they had slept in a hay barn. So far, they had not tangled with many Germans but this was only the start.

"Here's Carentan, Sir," said Howard, finding the last town on the list.

"Listen up, guys," the officer replied. "We landed here. Now we are right HERE, near this town, Isigny." Corporal Green prodded the map. "The D-Day landings were successful, but our troops have NOT taken as much territory as we had hoped. The battle lines are confused, and some of the terrain is tough going. It is IMPERATIVE that we move inland and claim as much ground as possible before the Germans counter-attack. They are movin' their strongest Panzer divisions into Normandy – AS WE SPEAK. The British Second Army, who landed further up the coast, are already havin' a hard time of it south of Bye-axe – sorry, Howard tells me that's B-a-y-e-u-x. We must help them some, but ALSO head west to help our fellow Americans who came in on Utah beach, north-west of here. Understood?"

The men exchanged looks that all meant the same thing – they understood. Corporal Green raised the map. He pointed to another town, linked to the sea by a channel of water. Its name was Carentan.

"I reckon we might be headin' here, real soon. This lil' town is held by the German 6th Paras, and they are tough sons of…"

A gate clicked open. Howard leaned forward on his stomach, raising his gun. The others did the same, staring at the gate that led into the orchard. A hand was pushing it forward. Seconds ticked away, then laughter rippled through the group and the soldiers lowered their machine-guns.

A deep *Moo!* announced the slow, easy arrival of three cows. They were a very unusual colour – white with grey speckles – and looked ancient. Walking in single file, they plodded through the orchard to a nearby field. One casually raised its tail and emptied its bowels with a splattery noise, to Rob's obvious disgust. Behind the cows walked a stooped old man. He saw the soldiers and waved his stick in greeting, but did not stop.

"Carentan is an important town," continued Corporal Green, dropping his voice to a whisper. "It's on a railway line that goes from the port of Cherbourg on the tip of Normandy, to Paris, capital of France. Carentan is also on this big road, from Cherbourg to Caen. See? Cherbourg is what the generals would call 'a major strategic objective'. We need it to get through supplies for our men. First, like I say, our guys have GOT to take Carentan."

He scanned the group, intently. "Now, I want you, Howard and Rob, to do a little scoutin' with me. Right now, there's someone we need to meet in Isigny. That person may have some helpful info'mation. After that, maybe tomorrow, the three of us will do some probin' near Carentan. We need to see where the Germans are buildin' up strength, and check out their supply lines. Without gettin' discovered or shot at, you understand. This is a recce mission – not heroics. You others can stay in Isigny, and will be given duties there.

"Another thing. How are those darn pigeons doin' anyway, Howard?"

"Fine, Sir," Howard replied.

"We'd better release them soon, or they won't be good for anything." A smile spread across the corporal's face. "Except eatin' that is."

His men snorted with laughter, all except Howard. The rations weren't so hot, but he didn't like Corporal Green's joke.

Paddy stirred, cocking his head at the noise. After two whole days in this tight basket the pigeons felt hot and miserable. Dizzy, too, with all that bumping around. How they longed to stretch their wings and fly. Free again.

Bouncer was scandalised. "Us – lunch!!"

"No, they need us for more important things," Paddy replied. "You'll see."

A brief jeep ride, and the three men and the pigeons arrived in the shattered town of Isigny. Howard gasped as they drove through the streets, nudging Rob a few times. Countless buildings had holes punched in them by mortar shells, or were pock-marked with bullets. Yet the local people were trying to go about their business, picking their way through chaos. One woman even had small milk churns attached to her bicycle and seemed to be delivering them. A Sherman tank overtook her, throwing up a cloud of choking dust. It was bizarre.

The jeep screeched to a halt. Jaws dropped as Corporal Green said:

"Now, how about a nice cup of coffee?"

22

Café Robert was on the corner of Isigny's main street. Buildings teetered all around, but miraculously the café was unscathed.

The Americans strode into its gloomy interior. A few customers – grizzle-haired men – were locked in a noisy discussion. One man was waving his arms dramatically. Silence fell as the elderly men inspected the newcomers, especially Corporal Green's dark skin and powerful build. 'Not a great welcome,' Howard thought. Then he remembered the destruction outside, and felt sorry for these old-timers.

Madame Robert greeted the group with a broad smile. She had a dark, beautiful face and greying hair pulled into a bun. "*Ah, les Américains!*" she cried. "*Trois cafés?*"

Howard nodded, "*Oui.*"

They sat at a spindly-legged table near the door, away from the other customers. There, Madame Robert told her incredible story.

Until two days ago, when the Americans had captured Isigny, her café had been popular with German officers. Every morning at 11 o'clock, as regular as clockwork, the highest-ranking men would come for their coffee and pastries. Little did they know she spoke fluent German.

"They never deliberately spoke of the war," Madame Robert explained, "but sometimes they made – how you say – slips of the tongue. These details I pass to my Resistance contact in Isigny. 'E pass anything important to London, I think."

"Very good," said Corporal Green, admiring this woman's strong defiant gaze. "Were there many Germans in Isigny?"

"Several 'undred, maybe one thousand. Perhaps," she shrugged.

The corporal leaned forward, lowering his voice.

"Do you have any contacts near Care-antan? We need info'mation on enemy tank numbers. Their movements. That kinda' thing. Maybe one of your Resistance contacts could help?"

Madame Robert looked puzzled. "Care-antanne?" she asked.

"*Carentan*," Howard cut in.

"Yes, Carentan," Corporal Green said, smiling.

Madame Robert turned towards a door that led to the kitchen, and shouted:

"Yvette!"

"*J'arrive*," a little voice replied.

A dark-haired girl emerged from the café, and joined the table. She reminded Howard of Becky, and he grinned. She blushed, as teenagers do, and stood shyly by her mother's side.

"Yvette and her friends 'ave – how you say – *bicyclettes*. Sometimes they go for little tours in the evenings. They do messages for me, and bring back things from my brother's farm – milk, butter, et cetera. His name is Henri Blanc. He lives four miles from Carentan. 'E is very 'elpful," Madame Robert added, looking straight at Corporal Green.

She spoke to her daughter in rapid French, then spoke to Corporal Green again.

"Yvette says he is there *demain* – tomorrow. She cannot bring you. It is too dangerous. But, she can make you a map of all the little roads they take on their *bicyclettes*."

Corporal Green nodded. "Mercy boocoop, Yvette," he said, finding his only two words of French. Rummaging in his kit bag, he put a fistful of Hershey bars on the table. "For your pals. And thank you Madame Robert, for all your kind help."

Madame Robert smiled, then nodded at Yvette.

"Thank you. *Monsieur est bien bon* – very kind," the girl said, beaming a smile. She gave a graceful curtsey.

With that, the men scraped back their chairs and left.

23

Armed with Yvette's map, the trio sped out of Isigny the following morning. Away from the tiny oasis of US-held territory, towards Carentan and Monsieur Blanc's farm.

The tree-lined exit from the town gave way to flat fields and patches of marshy ground. Cows grazed in the crisp sunshine. A few raised their heads and gazed at the jeep, chewing reflectively. Howard stared back. He felt he was drinking in the landscape, trying to memorise every twist in the road and unusual rock or tree, just in case.

Corporal Green, Rob and himself were in the jeep. They could not bring the motor-bike, as all three men were needed for this mission. Corporal Green also said the Harley-Davidson was too noisy, in case they had to slip behind enemy lines. Howard sat in the back, wedged uncomfortably between the wicker basket, the food rations and a stack of light weapons. Green was in a bad mood, so Howard kept quiet.

The corporal had insisted on bringing the pigeons. A radio was a more direct way of sending news, but a signal might get intercepted. Pigeons were silent, secret messengers which made them perfect for this scouting work. These pigeons would not return to the 2nd AD's Normandy base camp with a message; they had been trained to do one thing – fly back to RAF Hurn. From there, the message could be relayed swiftly to the War Office, and back to the commanders in Normandy.

Howard peered into the basket. The six pigeons were

listless, and had barely pecked at their breakfast. Today was the start of their third day in captivity with the US First Army and they were fed up. 'Those pigeons sure looked distressed,' he thought, deciding to tell Green when he got the chance. Right now, the man had other things on his mind. Carentan lay twelve miles to the south-west, in enemy hands. They could run into a German patrol at any minute. The very thought made Howard's stomach churn. He tugged his lucky dollar, rasping it back and forth along its chain as he studied the hand-written map.

A road loomed on their right. "Turn here, Sir," he hissed. The jeep swerved perilously as it left the main road, stones scattering under its tyres.

This route was narrower. Another turn, and the soldiers were on a bone-breaking track, not even wide enough for two vehicles. Thick, tall hedgerows lined either side of the rutted lane. A tangled mass of roots and vegetation, these hedgerows were at least ten feet high. At times, it seemed as if the track itself was sinking between two dark-green walls, like a river carving deep into an ancient forest.

"Creepy," Howard shouted in Rob's ear.

"Yep," he replied.

Corporal Green was silent, his eyes fixed ahead. As the jeep approached a sharp bend, the men tensed… but all was clear. The track was getting spookier by the minute. Howard looked at the map – it was just a mile to Monsieur Blanc's farm. 'This trip'd better be worth it,' he thought grimly.

He eyed the pigeons again. It struck him that fixing a message container on a pigeon's leg might be tricky. Pigeons were fragile, and sort of wild. What if they struggled, and he broke one of their legs by accident? He did not want to think about that. It was too awful.

The hedgerows seemed to grow even taller. The sound of thunder – or was it heavy artillery fire? – rumbled in the distance.

Corporal Green dropped a gear and turned yet another corner, only to see the tail of a tank disappearing round the next bend. It was just fifty yards away, and it was not one of theirs. "Holy Smoke!" he breathed.

"Back up, back up!" yelled Howard.

Slamming the jeep into reverse, Green shot back down the lane, then revved through an open gateway. It led into a tiny field bordered by more towering hedgerows. As Howard and Rob clutched their rifles, Corporal Green drove right under the branches of a thick, overhanging tree and halted jerkily, just inches from its trunk. He switched off the engine. "Phew, that was close," Green whispered. He fell silent, but you could almost hear him thinking.

"Howard," he said at last. "We must be right beside this man's farm. You speak the French lingo. Get yourself down to Monsieur Blanc, pronto. Take the pigeons. Find out what you can. If he tells you anythin' useful, release a few. Don't hang around."

Howard was stunned, but he just said: "Yes, Sir!"

If the map was correct, the farmhouse was barely a quarter of a mile away to the right. Howard eased the pigeon basket off the back seat. With a pounding heart, he crept along the track, following in the path of the German tank. To his huge relief, he saw a leafy driveway ahead on his right, closer than he had expected.

A stone farmhouse sat in a belt of trees. Howard was going to knock on the front door, but thought better of it. Instead, he slipped into a yard surrounded by crumbling outhouses. From one shed, he heard the rhythmical *fff - fff - fff* of milk streaming into a metal pail. Stepping inside, he saw a stockily-built farmer on a stool, sitting next to a cow.

"Monsieur Blanc?" he asked.

The farmer looked up. If he was surprised to see a young American soldier in his cow-shed that morning, he did not show it. Monsieur Blanc's leathery face creased into a smile. He had his sister's strong features, and the same frank eyes.

"*Bienvenu* – Welcome!" he whispered

"*Merci*," Howard replied.

The farmer put his left index finger to his lips, and gestured dramatically with his other hand. Howard understood that he had to get away from the door. The man must have also heard the tank, even though he was milking his cow as if nothing had happened.

The young soldier walked towards him, but left the pigeon basket by the half-open door. A cool breeze sifted through the wicker-work, and the pigeons lifted their wings gratefully.

"Ah, the pigeons," the farmer whispered. "You 'ave a message you wish to send?"

Howard nodded. Wasting no time, he explained the mission and how Madame Robert had given them her brother's name. Did Monsieur Blanc have any news on enemy troop movements or their supply lines?

He certainly did. The farmer had seen a lot that day as he had trudged around his little holding. In the morning, returning from the orchard with a basket of apples, he had spotted German foot-soldiers. Heading for Carentan, he was sure. Just before milking the cow, he had observed five tanks roll down the lane – the ones that Corporal Green had almost run into. He thought they were Panzers, rather than the deadly Tiger tanks. Yet nobody had come into his yard until now. The Germans had let him be, thinking that he was just an ageing farmer with a few cows and apple trees. They were wrong, of course.

"You are certain the tanks were going to Carentan?" Howard asked.

"*Oui*. And more will come, I think. This is a very dangerous place for you," the farmer replied.

Howard took a deep breath. Any information of this sort was vital and had to be sent back to England immediately. Digging into his pockets, he found a pencil and note-pad. The thin paper was over-stamped with the words:

OPERATIONAL MESSAGE – Telephone to War Office Signal Office, WHITEHALL 9400

Frantically, he scribbled the details on the message paper, adding his own name and the date – June 11th, 1944. He wrote a second identical message. Next he got two bright green message containers. These were also very light, made of *papier-mâché*. With fumbling fingers, Howard rolled one message into a cigarette shape and folded it in two. He inserted it into the tiny container and popped the lid shut. He did the same with the second message.

Now for the pigeons. He opened a small trap-door on the basket lid and fished inside with his hand. Grabbing a pigeon at random, he pulled out a brown-and-white hen called Jewel and shut the door quickly. His jerky movements scared her, especially when he tried to fix the tiny strip of webbing that held the container around her leg. Jewel braced her wings and struggled. Howard's fingers clamped on her skinny, strawberry-coloured leg.

"*Attention!*" the farmer warned, stepping forward. He took the pigeon from Howard. Cupping the bird's belly in his right hand, he deftly tucked her two legs between his strong fingers. He placed his left hand over her body, and she grew calm.

"*Merci*," whispered Howard. The young American secured the webbing around her leg, snapping shut the popper that held it tight. The message container was now snugly in place. Taking the bird back from Monsieur Blanc, Howard moved to the open door-way.

One, two, three – he tossed her high into the air. A clattering noise, and she was gone. He repeated this process with a second bird, while Monsieur Blanc nodded approvingly. Just as Howard released her, they heard the sound of an engine.

Both men froze. Once again, Monsieur Blanc put a finger to his lips. Howard nodded, but tapped his watch in reply. Yes, they had to be quiet but time was running out. He must return to the jeep.

"I have to go. You have been very kind," he said quietly.

The farmer shook his hand.

Howard checked his watch. Almost half an hour had gone by. Resisting the urge to run, he stole down the driveway. Back on the rutted track, he scanned both directions quickly, then sneaked towards the field. He dashed to the tree where Corporal Green had parked the jeep. Lifting a low-hanging branch, he stared in utter disbelief. The jeep had gone.

24

The basket now contained four pigeons: Paddy, Bouncer, Star and Cockney Blue. To their amazement, it seemed as if Howard had started chasing through the field. The motion shook them like rag dolls but, mercifully, the jolting soon stopped. The pigeons felt a soft thud as the basket landed on a patch of wet grass.

"My turn next," Bouncer panted. "I get to fly next."

"You'll be lucky," Cockney Blue replied. "This lad's lost 'is head.

"Is he crying?" Paddy asked, hearing a strange noise.

"No, not quite," Bouncer replied.

Howard knelt beside them, burying his face in his hands. Deep shuddering breaths wracked his body. He was trying to think, trying to focus. His mind raced: Why did the guys leave? Did more Germans come? Maybe Rob and Green were hiding in a field, just down the track? Maybe he was in the wrong field…!

As panic subsided, a feeling of strange calm seeped into his body. Howard remembered Sergeant Glower's words that day in England: "Do your job! DO YOUR JOB." These words now rang in his head, not panicky questions that he could not answer. He was a trained soldier, a volunteer, in a recce unit of the 2nd Armored Division 'Hell on Wheels'. This was just another challenge – a test of nerves and skill.

He decided to go back to Monsieur Blanc's farm, to tell him what had happened and maybe give him one of the pigeons. After that, he would skirt along the track towards

Isigny. He was just inside enemy lines. A few miles and he would be safe, back in Allied-held territory.

He hurried back to the farm, and met Monsieur Blanc who was leaving the barn with a pail full of milk. This time the farmer was very surprised to see him.

"Stay 'ere. In the barn. Leave when it is dark," he begged, after Howard had told him about the jeep.

Howard refused, but gratefully accepted a cup of cool milk from a nearby churn. "I must go. My friends are waiting, somewhere," he said. Then he remembered his plan to leave the farmer a pigeon in case he had more news to send. Pointing to the basket he said:

"*Prenez-en un* – take one."

Monsieur Blanc disappeared into a corner of the cow shed. He returned with a small metal cage. It had droppings and feathers stuck to it. Howard scooped his hand into the wicker basket and pulled out the third pigeon of the day. This time it was Bouncer.

The young man bundled an indignant Bouncer into the grubby cage, and handed the farmer a message container and a few sheets of paper. Then he waved another hasty good-bye and left.

Minutes later he was back in the field that the jeep had left so mysteriously. Deep ridges in the earth told him that the vehicle had reversed swiftly and spun out of the narrow gateway heading towards Isigny. Howard decided to stay inside the fields and make his way back towards the main Carentan-Isigny road until he found the others. The hedgerows were so dense, he had no choice but to walk by the ditch and slip into the undergrowth at any sign of danger. It was scary. Now he knew how an animal felt when it was being hunted.

There were few gates in these small fields. In each corner Howard had to climb gingerly onto the bank and battle through to the next, equally tiny field. This was ancient *bocage* country, and these dense hedgerows had been lain down centuries ago to divide up the pasture-land. Howard was soon weary and covered with scratches.

Spotting a sturdy ash tree, he put down the pigeon basket and climbed up for a better view. Open ground stretched on the other side of the track, parts of it shimmering in the light. 'A marsh,' Howard thought. Scrambling still higher, he spotted a ribbon of grey. It was the main road they had taken that morning from Isigny. Following it with his gaze, he was stunned by what he saw. Pulling across that road, at the very turning where Corporal Green had swerved so violently, was a German tank. Soldiers swarmed around it, like angry bees defending their queen.

Howard almost fell out of the tree in shock.

He saw more tanks, turning in single file onto the lane. Heading towards him. Perhaps they were taking the back roads to Carentan, like the other German tanks? He stared in mounting horror. Already, he could hear the harsh clang of metal on stone as they drew closer and closer along the track.

Howard gripped the tree tightly. At least his body was camouflaged by thick foliage but – what about the pigeon basket? Glancing down, he saw one of its brown corners pointing up in the air, clearly visible on the ground. He stared at the basket, then at the track, thinking: 'They'll see it. They'll see it.'

Just as he started shimmying down the tree, he heard the crunch of boots approaching the bend a few yards away. Howard yanked himself back up, seconds before a group of soldiers loped around the corner and into view. They ran down the track right underneath him. At a signal from an officer, they stabbed a section of ditch with their bayonets. Howard clung to his tree trunk, knowing that his life depended on it. Looking over at the marsh again, he saw a cluster of trees and a half-ruined farmhouse. When he got out of this scrape, he would head over there – if he got out of here, that is.

Now the tanks were grinding and sloshing down the track. Perhaps they were Tiger tanks. Howard was not sure, but he counted each monster as it passed under his hiding place: One, two, three…seven tanks in all! It took an eternity for them to pass. Howard shut his eyes. He thought of his Mom. He tried to think of a silent prayer, but could only manage: 'Please God, let me get out of here. Please God, let me get out of here.'

The last tank passed. More foot-soldiers rushed by, bristling with weapons. At last, they rounded the next bend and before long all was quiet, once again. The air grew heavy and still. Howard waited, his heart still pounding. A bead of sweat trickled from his brow, but he dared not wipe it off. He breathed in deeply.

Into that tense silence, broke a magical sound. It was the carolling song of a blackbird from a nearby tree. Like water flashing over stones, the voice trembled sweetly. The bird stopped, then sang once more. Howard listened, grateful. When the song had finished, he eased his way down the tree and onto the hedgerow's solid bank. Conscious of every twig-crack and slurp of mud under his boots, he picked up the basket and climbed down onto the track, towards the marsh and the ruined farmhouse.

"Gotta go, guys!" he whispered.

25

After wading through the mosquito-ridden wetland, Howard approached the ruined farmhouse.

It was ringed by the overgrown hedge of a wild garden. He ducked beside the hedge and scanned the driveway. Nothing moved. All was quiet, except for the sleepy droning of bees from an ancient rose bush. The sun beat down on his shoulder blades. Howard felt thirsty. He needed to get inside, and rest. Besides, he had to write another message – urgently.

He inspected the farmhouse. Made of cut stone, it was clearly deserted. Two grimy windows flanked a wooden door, one of which was broken. Peering inside, Howard could just make out a kitchen, its floor strewn with rubbish and glass. At least there was a table, plus an old wooden chair. He reached for the door. Turning the knob, he pushed. The door was stuck. Heaving with his shoulder, he pushed harder.

As it burst inwards, he felt a sideways blow, as someone dived on him. Howard hit the floor with a painful crash. A bayonet stabbed at his chest, pinning him to the ground. His attacker had mad glinting eyes and a shaven head, with a ragged crest of hair down the middle.

"Rob!" he gasped.

"Why if it ain't the pigeon man," Corporal Green growled, from a corner of the room.

The two men hauled him to his feet and dusted him down. Rob kept saying, "Gee, I'm so sorry, Howard. I thought it was one of them…!" Then, in an urgent whisper, Corporal Green explained what had happened back at the field. When Howard had been gone a while, Rob had also done a spot of tree climbing. That was when he had seen Tiger tanks and troops further back along the road from Isigny. Rob had also noticed the ruined farmhouse, fringed with trees. Corporal Green had decided to pull out of the field, and hide the jeep close to the main road, in case their escape route was cut off.

"We figured you'd make it back here," Corporal Green said, eyeing Howard. "And you did."

"Yep," he replied, avoiding the corporal's gaze.

"Rations guys?" Green said, handing out packs to Rob and Howard.

"There's no doubt all those tanks and troops are headed for Carentan," he continued, opening his own pack. "Tomorrow at dawn – June 12th – word is that our guys from the 101st Airborne are due to attack Carentan. Two things may happen. Either they'll find more German soldiers there than they'd bargained for, or," he paused, "those Tiger tanks will hit the town with a counter-attack later in the day." He looked at Howard.

"How many pigeons have you got left, son?"

"Three, sir," Howard replied. He explained how he had left Bouncer with Monsieur Blanc.

"Release another two with a message now," Green ordered. "We'll hold one bird back, in case we need him. We gotta' try and leave here, tonight, if the coast is clear. Back to Isigny."

They ate, and swigged cool water from their canteens. Howard flicked crumbs into the pigeons' food tray, as he had no corn to give them. When the crumbs were gone, Howard poured in water from his canteen. Meanwhile, Corporal

Green scribbled the messages, each warning about the extra seven Tiger tanks heading on the back roads to Carentan.

A breeze drifted through the broken window, and a distinctive sound filled the air. It was the soft cry of a wood pigeon, calling from a nearby tree. 'Pro-proo-proo, pro-pro' it repeated. Howard's three remaining pigeons stirred, perhaps recognising their wild cousin's call.

"Ready, Sir?" Howard asked.

He pulled a pigeon out of the basket. It was Star, an iron-grey bird. Holding the pigeon firmly, Howard got Rob to fix on the message container. The pigeon accepted it meekly. Stepping to the window, Howard released him without any problem. The second bird, Cockney Blue, struggled briefly but Howard got the container in place. Sweeping over the driveway, Cockney Blue also left in a flurry of wings. A single black-and-white pigeon – the one Howard had somehow imagined as Becky's favourite – was left in the basket.

Nothing to do now, but hunker by the wall and wait.

Night fell at last. A pale moon rose above the trees, casting a silvery glow over the marshland. Corporal Green kept checking his watch, and taking quick looks out the window. He eyed the road to Isigny. At 2 o'clock in the morning, as the others were dozing off, he rose to his feet, stiffly.

"Wake up, you guys," he snapped. "Maybe it's time to make a run for it. Rob, go see if the coast is clear. Check out the jeep."

Rob yawned, and struggled up without a word. Easing the door towards him, he slipped into the night. There was a faint rustle from the pigeon basket; Paddy was also awake.

"Do you think those birds are goin' to make it back to

England?" Corporal Green asked, breaking the silence. "Maybe we should've brought the radio." He sighed deeply. "I just hope we get outta' this fix before too long."

"Yes sirree," Howard agreed.

It seemed like another age passed.

"Where the hell is Rob? I keep losing you guys today," said Green. Howard felt his head droop again. He slipped into a dreamless sleep.

The door jerked open. Howard woke with a fright. Rob stood there, breathless. It was already daylight. Corporal Green was snoring lightly, hugging his rifle.

"Where have you been?" Howard exclaimed.

"Jeez, it's a shark pool out there!" Rob burst out. "The place is swimming with Germans. I couldn't get back. There were sentries out on the road – I've been hiding in a ditch all night. These must be reinforcements headin' for that town, what-you-call-it, Car-antan? I think the jeep's okay, but we're stuck here. You better get a message strapped to your pigeon – and fast."

Howard searched for the message pad and pencil, while Rob woke Green.

"Corporal, at least another six tanks have passed through," Rob whispered urgently. "The place is surrounded by Germans."

Corporal Green stirred. "What?"

Rob repeated what he had just said.

"Time to let the last pigeon go then," Corporal Green hissed. "Howard, you write this–"

"I'm already doin' that, Sir!"

"Well, step on it, son. Tell me what you saw, Rob."

As Rob briefed the corporal, Howard finished his message.

It read:

> June 12th, 05.40hrs. Our three-man recce team in ruined farmhouse on right just after junction, five miles due west of Isigny, on road to Carentan. Behind enemy lines. Further build-up of enemy troops, including six tanks during the night. They are heading for Carentan. We may need assistance here. Please advise 2nd Armored of our position.
>
> Pvt. Howard Jones, Recce Team, 82nd Battalion, 2nd AD.

"Show me," Green said. He read the message, then grunted his approval. "Good work, son."

After stuffing the message in the last container, Howard opened the basket. The black-and-white bird was mooching in the corner, looking sorry for himself. 'He'll never make it back,' Howard thought glumly, reaching in his hand.

This time, Howard fixed on the message container while Rob held the bird. Paddy started to strain in Rob's hands. "Watch out!" Corporal Green called. Howard leaned towards his buddy, and took Paddy in the classic loftman's grip – just as Monsieur Blanc had shown him.

Paddy's brain was churning. 'Must go, must go. Must fly.'

But his body stilled. Howard moved to the open window, holding the bird so firmly he could feel its thudding heart, yet so softly its feathers were like satin in his fingers.

"Now boy," Howard whispered. "Home. Fly home."

Stretching his arms, he thrust Paddy through the broken panes, forgetting that a German sniper might see them both. He opened his palms, and the bird was free. He willed Paddy skywards, as the pigeon spun in a huge circle and crested the trees before disappearing from view. No gunshots rang out, just the clatter of a pigeon's wings that echoed in the still morning.

Paddy flew with strong, steady wing-beats.

"Home," he thought. "Home."

26

Paddy felt glad to be out of the confining basket. But he was tired. Winging over the driveway that led from the old farmhouse, he accidently clipped a tree. Sparrows burst from its branches, cheeping indignantly.

At the base of that tree, the US army jeep was still hidden in dense undergrowth. Later, when the German troops had moved on, the three Americans would dash for safety, down the road to Isigny.

A weak sun battled through the clouds. It cast a warm, gentle glow over Normandy. Paddy could now see the mosaic of tiny little fields, each surrounded by hedgerows like the ones Howard had struggled through yesterday. Some of the hedgerows were barely fifty yards apart, great coils of vegetation that teemed with life. For the first few miles, they stood proud and undamaged. Further north, where Allied and German troops had clashed, he saw others with huge gashes cut through them. Freshly-ripped branches, and tracks carved deep into the buttery earth told of violent assaults by mortar shells and tanks. On one hedgerow, Paddy saw a tank tilted upright, its soft under-belly exposed. This tank had tried to break into the next field, but had taken a direct hit instead. A soldier lay dead on its metal casing.

In some hedgerows, soldiers hid like rabbits, burrowed into the greenery. Some were German, others British or American. Many were scared and wanted no part in this war.

Paddy kept his thoughts on flying, until he heard the unmistakable *tat-tat-tat-tat* of machine-guns. Soldiers were trading gunfire in a village a mile ahead. There was a sudden explosion, then another. Orange flame spat from the ground, followed by a gush of smoke. Wounded men cried in pain. To the west, at Carentan, a fiercer battle was now raging between the German troops holding the town and the men of the 101st Airborne Division.

The pigeon veered east, spooked by the noise. Skirting more bullets, he flew blindly off-course. When he had steadied himself, he flew straight and true. Paddy had an urgent message; he had to get home by the shortest route. After twenty minutes of hard flying, he saw a glinting mass of water and a strip of pale sand. The beaches of Normandy!

A few wing-flaps and Paddy was directly over a section of coast. Black smoke wisped from the wreck of a burning tank. Twisted metal lay heaped near a sea wall. But all seemed calm, as the sea lapped quietly over the golden sand.

Barely out to sea, Paddy felt a whoosh at his shoulder.

"Bouncer!" he called.

"No breakfast, and look at me!" Bouncer replied. He did a crazy loop in the air, righting himself just above the waves.

"I've got a message, too," quipped Bouncer. "From our farmer friend."

Bouncer was in 'flying form', as Mr. Hughes would say, clearly delighted to see his brother. They flew together, over the aquamarine surf. The sun lit a path in the water, guiding them forward. Flying in daylight on this glorious morning was simple, compared to some of their flights at RAF Ballykelly and RAF Hurn. Exhaustion would be their biggest enemy.

An hour out to sea, a small flock of pigeons surged towards them. Perhaps ten or more, weaving a flight path with fresh, strong wings. Each bird had a green container strapped to its leg. These birds were flying back to a civilian pigeon loft.*

"Where did you fly from?" Paddy cried.

"From a boat, a boat," one repeated.

"And where are you going?" asked Bouncer.

"To England, up the coast," replied another.

The pigeons flew as one flock, until their paths would have to separate. These birds were flying due north-east, while Paddy and Bouncer would have to veer north-west for RAF Hurn.

They drew close to a ship. Glancing down, the pigeons saw men lying on its broad deck. Some were badly injured, with bandages on their arms, legs and even their heads. They were returning to hospital in England. Despite their injuries, a few men cheered as the pigeons zoomed overhead. Paddy wanted to rest on the ship's mast, but knew he could not.

Each wing-beat was like the stroke of a machine: whoosh, whoosh, whoosh, bringing them closer to shore. The pigeons had to keep going.

About a mile from the ship, they saw a flock of black-backed gulls, squabbling over kitchen scraps in the water.

"Breakfast," called one pigeon. Foolishly, he dipped towards the waves. "No!" Paddy called, knowing that pigeons could not dive as gulls can. Their feathers were not designed for that. Besides, the gulls had an evil look on their faces. They rose from the sea, threatening to mob the pigeon. He flapped in panic, avoiding one gull as it lunged towards him. Paddy saw the gulls' curved beaks, and powerful wings. He feared they would scatter the entire pigeon flock.

* A privately-owned loft, whose owners kept NPS pigeons

At a call from Paddy, the pigeons rose like bomber pilots, away from the milling gang. The pigeon who had fancied a take-away changed his mind, making a swift get-away instead.

The pigeons were still in good spirits, weaving through the air. A tail wind gently pushed them home, the air a delicious mix of warm and cool currents and scented with a salty tang. The patterned sea shone brightly, with patches of darker shadow.

But flying became harder, the further they flew over the mesmeric expanse of water. The pigeons' wings weakened, and a few birds were perilously close to the cresting waves. One skimmed the water at times, utterly exhausted. His feathers soon had a crusting of salt, and he flew ever more slowly. Finally, he tumbled into the sea like a discarded toy. Others would follow. Perhaps a third of these pigeons would not make it back to the loft with their messages.

The birds flew on, and on and on. They spied more ships, these ones heading for Normandy with fresh troops and food supplies.

Over four hours had passed; the flock flew grimly on. Paddy felt hypnotised by the drumming of wing beats and the endless stretch of sea. It was like a mirror, flat and shiny. He was on auto-pilot, with his eyes fixed ahead. The horizon was traced with lines, and Paddy wavered briefly over which flight path to follow. Below him, another two birds, exhausted and longing to feel solid earth beneath their feet, dropped into the waves.

A strong swell rose on the water, rolling towards the home shores of England. Just as the flock reached dry land, the pigeons divided into their two groups. Paddy and Bouncer veered north-west for RAF Hurn; the others continued up the English coast. The RAF Hurn birds were seasoned flyers – they would not repeat the mistake they had made on their first flight from Slemish Hill.

At RAF Hurn, Mike swept the ground with vigorous strokes. It had been five days since Paddy and Bouncer had been shipped off to the US First Army. He had almost given up hope of seeing them alive again.

He paused as Sergeant McLean strode towards him.

"Mike," the sergeant said. "I've a feeling that we might get another pigeon back very soon. I've just got a garbled message from Whitehall. They want to know the second a bird hits the deck. Stay near the loft, will you?"

"Yes-sir," Mike replied. He dragged the heavy brush towards the loft. Inside, Princess and the chicks were waiting in their nest box, and the air was full of fluttering birds.

*   *   *

Paddy pushed ahead of Bouncer. He swooped over a crest of jagged rocks, and the railings of a promenade. This was Bournemouth. With a huge effort the two birds surged up and over the town's bustling streets. Higher, higher, they flew, above the criss-cross of roads and terraced houses. Then came a stretch of velvety countryside, the sudden sparkle of a river. A fence marked the boundary of RAF Hurn, with its concrete flatness.

Paddy zoomed straight to his loft. Lowering his tired legs and fanning his tail feathers, he dropped onto the landing board. Folding his wings neatly, he stepped through the bars.

Mike spotted the black-and-white plumage of Sergeant McLean's favourite pigeon. In the distance, he could see a second, iron-grey bird still flying gamely towards his home. This one he was not so certain of, as so many pigeons were grey, but it looked like Paddy's cheeky brother. Hurling down his yard brush, he yelped with joy. "Paddy's back, Sir! Maybe Bouncer, too!"

Sergeant McLean broke into a run. Seconds later, they were reading the vital message that Paddy had brought from France.

27

Postscript: September 1st, 1944. 6 o'clock

Moyleen Lofts, Carnlough, Co. Antrim. Andrew Hughes is
waiting for the evening news on the BBC's Home Service. He
has finished the pigeons for the day, and is enjoying a well-
earned cup of tea. The radio emits a series of pips:

"Here is the News, read by Joseph MacLeod.

*The Americans have entered France's most famous
fortress town – Verdun. Already, they have three
bridgeheads over the Meuse – the last big river before
the German frontier. To the north, our forces are only
ten miles from the Belgian border. British troops are
following up their great Somme drive without pause."*

The phone rings. Andrew Hughes puts down his teacup,
and picks up the receiver.

"It's Sergeant McLean, chief loftman RAF Hurn," a voice

crackles down the line. "Have you heard, Mr. Hughes? Your Paddy's a hero."

"Aye?" Mr Hughes replies.

"I have to report to you that Paddy will be getting a special honour this evening. A very special honour," Sergeant McLean says, in his light Scottish drawl.

"Is that so?"

"Yes, he is being awarded a medal for bravery, the Dickin medal. Can I read you the official citation?"

"Please do,' says Mr. Hughes, sitting down.

The officer begins:

> " 'Of the several hundreds of pigeons, both service and civilian, used in the Normandy invasion operations, 'Paddy' accomplished the fastest recorded time with a message in 4 hours 50 minutes. Bred in Northern Ireland, Paddy worked on air/sea rescue training and operations on a Northern Ireland RAF station from May 1943 until March 1944. On March 15th he was transferred to a south coast RAF station, at which he was 'settled' by March 23rd, and had completed his re-training and standard tests at the new station by May 28th.
> An exceptionally intelligent pigeon.' "

Silence falls. "One question," Mr. Hughes asks softly, after a long pause. "Will Paddy be coming back home?"

"Most certainly, but right now he has guest appearances to make – at a few pigeon shows. I guess you know all about that sort of thing," the officer adds with a chuckle. "We'll get him, and his new family, back to you in no time. And Bouncer, of course."

The phones clicks down. Annie Hughes looks at her husband questioningly. He turns to speak to her.

"Annie, you'll never believe…"

THE END

Historical Note

Just as the Victoria Cross is awarded to soldiers for bravery, the Dickin Medal is awarded to animals. The idea came from Maria Dickin, founder of the Peoples' Dispensary for Sick Animals in Britain. Since 1943, when she established the award to recognise the service of animals from World War II onwards, fifty-five Dickin Medals have been awarded to:

The Dickin Medal

- 32 pigeons
- 19 dogs
- 3 horses
- 1 cat

Why so many medals for pigeons, you might ask? About 200,000 pigeons served in Britain during WWII, the vast majority with the National Pigeon Service. They delivered vital messages when it was often the sole means of communication, flying at speeds of up to a mile per minute. They struggled through all weathers, even when badly wounded and exhausted, to deliver their messages. Pigeons saved airmen lost at sea, acted as couriers for the French Resistance and rescued soldiers trapped behind enemy lines. Through this work, they saved hundreds - possibly thousands - of lives.

The Dickin Medal bears the words "For Gallantry" and "We Also Serve", surrounded by a laurel wreath. It is made of bronze, and the ribbon is striped in green, dark brown and pale blue to represent water, earth and air.

Only one Irish animal has ever won the Dickin Medal. That animal was a bird – a pigeon named Paddy.

He was bred by Andrew Hughes, a famous pigeon breeder who lived in the seaside village of Carnlough, Co. Antrim, Northern Ireland. Mr. Hughes was born on June 10th, 1880, one of eleven brothers and sisters. When Paddy was hatched, around March 1943,

Paddy the Pigeon

Mr. Andrew Hughes

Mr. Hughes was then sixty-two years old. He had served in WWI, 1914-1918, reaching the rank of captain, and had travelled widely in Europe.

Andrew Hughes led a quiet, almost reclusive, life in Carnlough with his wife Annie. They had nieces and nephews, but no children. Mr. Hughes did the accounts for local businesses, was a Justice of the Peace and treasurer of Carnlough Methodist Church. He also had a thriving business; breeding and training pigeons at his famed Moyleen Lofts. He specialised in the Putman strain, descended from birds that he had bought from a loft in Belgium. Mr. Hughes raced his pigeons between Ireland and Wales, and regularly advertised his stock in pigeon journals.

Paddy was a handsome black-and-white pigeon, described in pigeon terms as a 'dark chequer gay pied cock'. His National Pigeon Service number was NPS-43-9451.

Records show that Paddy first served in RAF Ballykelly, in Northern Ireland, on Air/Sea rescue missions from May 1943 until March 1944. He was transferred to RAF Hurn, then in Hampshire, on March 15th, 1944. Within eight days he was 'settled', and completed his re-training just in time to serve during the Normandy Landings.

Paddy was a favourite of his loftman in RAF Hurn, believed to be a Sergeant McLean. This man may also have

Pigeon parachute, WWII at Bletchley Park, Milton Keynes.

worked with Paddy in RAF Ballykelly, according to a leading Northen Irish pigeon man, John McMullan, a neighbour of Andrew Hughes in Carnlough.

And what of the Normandy landings? Several hundred pigeons went to France, but not all were released on D-Day itself. They were given tasks with secret code-names: A1, P1, P2, U1 and U2. Paddy was one of thirty birds delivered by RAF Hurn to operational units of the First US Army on June 8th, 1944, for the task called 'U2'. He was released at around 8.15a.m. on June 12th in Normandy, after four days in captivity. The weather conditions were good.

He returned to his loft in just 4 hours and 50 minutes – the fastest recorded time during the Normandy Landings. He was awarded a Dickin Medal for this achievement on September 1st, 1944. We do not know where he was released, or the content of his message.

American soldiers landing at Omaha, post D-Day

However, he may have been shipped to Omaha beach with a unit of the 2nd Armored Division, First US Army, which landed there on June 9th. The 2nd Armored Division (a tank division, nick-named 'Hell on Wheels') soon played an important part in the Normandy campaign, after it was ordered to help the 101st Airborne Division (US Army) in its defence of a town called Carentan.

The 101st Airborne, made famous by the book and mini-series, *Band of Brothers*, seized Carentan at dawn on June 12th. The very next day, German troops staged a fierce counter-attack. But the Allies were prepared. Code-breakers in Bletchley Park, England, had intercepted radio messages sent by the German Army. Who knows what part pigeon messengers may also have played in this drama...

Moyleen Lofts

A. S. HUGHES

"MOYLEEN"

Carnlough, Northern Ireland

Home of the Famous Hughes-Putmans

Homing World Stud Book, 1948

After the war, Paddy returned to Mr. Hughes in Carnlough as a hero. His owner was clearly proud of him, and featured his photo in ads for the Moyleen Lofts.

Dickin Medal winner, Paddy the Pigeon, lived until the ripe old age - for pigeons, that is - of eleven.

Did You Know?

Paddy's Dickin Medal went up for auction in Dublin in 1999. It was bought by an Irish pigeon-fancier and FCA Commandant Kevin Spring for almost stg£7,000

Acknowledgements

Many people helped in the research for this book.

They include Kevin Spring, Col. Leo Brownen and Tony Kehoe, all pigeon enthusiasts who helped with archival information about Paddy, or in relation to pigeons in war. Denis White of the Clontarf RPC generously gave me access to both his loft in Clontarf and his books, and also read the manuscript. My thanks to the staff in the Defence Forces press office, the Met Office and Liam O'Dwyer of the Marine Rescue Co-ordination Centre for their help with technical details. Also to Robert Dunbar, who kindly assisted with the nuances of Co. Antrim speech; and to fellow children's writer, Larry O'Loughlin, for his kind suggestions. My thanks also to Aisling, Marion and Sherry for their valuable inputs.

In Northern Ireland, special thanks are due to pigeon men Bill Reid and Joe Patterson, and to Mr. Reid's daughter, Elizabeth. Veteran pigeon fancier, John McMullan of Carnlough, and the Rev. Andrew Wilson of Glenarm Presbyterian Church, helped greatly with research during and after my visit to Paddy's home-place. My thanks also to Ann Dunlop for her research on Andrew Hughes, and to local historian John Montgomery who helped with vital details for this story.

In England, I received courteous assistance from the staff at Bletchley Park Museum, home to the Pigeons at War collection. I was also greatly helped during my visit by Colin Hill, of the Bletchley and Milton Keynes Homing Society.

Thanks are also due to Mike Phipp, historian of Bournemouth International Airport, and the staff of the Public Records Office, the Imperial War Museum (photo on page 120) and the Royal Air Force Museum, Hendon, in particular Nina Burls. The BBC news bulletins used on pages 3, 16 and 112 were kindly provided by the BBC's Written Archives Centre.

My thanks to the editor and staff of the *Racing Pigeon* and *Homing Gazette* for their assistance and to all readers who replied to my requests for information, especially keen pigeon fancier, Derek Castle. Also to Andy Bevan, of IA Bookshops in Birmingham for his help.

Margaret Roberta Ervine-Burger of the Hughes family, kindly gave permission to use Mr. Hughes's photograph on page 118. Together with other members of his family, she was most helpful and gave this project her blessing. My thanks to Kevin Spring, owner of Paddy's Dickin Medal, who kindly provided the photo for page 117.

Also, to the Pensions Board, who afforded me the space to produce this book over a four-year period.

Finally to three teachers who nurtured my love of history: Professor Geoffrey Best, who was warmly supportive of this project, Professor John Röhl and Maurice Hutt.

My ultimate thanks are due to Pierce, for his huge support and considerable input into the book.

AVAILABLE BY POST

paddy
THE PIGEON

ORDER FORM

	Price*	No. of copies
Ireland	€7.00	………..
United Kingdom	£5.50	………..
Europe	€7.50	…………
North America	US$8	…………

* Price includes postage and packaging.

NAME...

ADDRESS ....
....
....
....
Payment enclosed...................................(please fill in amount)

Please send cheque/euro giro/money order to:

PIXIE BOOKS
72 Cabra Park, Phibsboro, Dublin 7, Ireland
www.pixiebooks.ie

ALSO AVAILABLE FROM PIXIE BOOKS

BRUSH

A Tale of Two Foxes
by Pierce Feiritear
(Age Group: 6- to 10-year-olds)

Misty and Ash are two hungry young foxes, and they're determined
to get food for their family. But they also have to out-fox an ugly
hound called Raptor, and his nasty scheming owners, the MacLugs.
Can they do it?

"Animal stories for young readers don't come better than this…Great
fun." (INIS, Children's Books Ireland Magazine)

"Fast, furious and warmly humorous. …Good readers, reluctant
readers and well established readers will enjoy this tale."
(INTOUCH, Primary Teachers' Journal)

ORDER FORM

	Price*	No. of copies
Ireland	€6	………..
United Kingdom	£5.00	………..
Europe	€7	………….
North America	US$8	………….

* Price includes postage and packaging.

NAME...

ADDRESS ....

....

....

....

Payment enclosed..................................(please fill in amount)

Please send cheque/euro giro/money order to:
PIXIE BOOKS
72 Cabra Park, Phibsboro, Dublin 7, Ireland
www.pixiebooks.ie